# Maren pushed open the door.

Two things registered for her at once. The first was that the bed was very large and very pink, and was in fact exactly the bed that she had specified be put in her room—the bed that she had always dreamed of.

A princess bed.

To go with a princess castle.

The second was that there was a *man* on it. *Lounging.*

He was—she could see even though he was lying down—very tall. And he was wearing a black suit, and his black hair was pushed off of his forehead in a devilish fashion.

His eyes were black and far too sharp. And she knew beyond a shadow of a doubt that she would remember this moment, and this image, with startling clarity forever.

There was something intense that radiated from him.

Something she could feel, burning deep within her chest, but not something that she could name.

She froze.

It was like looking at a predator. A small voice inside of her whispered *run.*

But another voice, just as compelling, whispered *stay.*

# Millie Adams

—

## THE CHRISTMAS THE GREEK CLAIMED HER

**HARLEQUIN**
## PRESENTS

Recycling programs
for this product may
not exist in your area.

ISBN-13: 978-1-335-59298-9

The Christmas the Greek Claimed Her

Copyright © 2023 by Millie Adams

For questions and comments about the quality of this book,
please contact us at CustomerService@Harlequin.com.

Harlequin Enterprises ULC
22 Adelaide St. West, 41st Floor
Toronto, Ontario M5H 4E3, Canada
www.Harlequin.com

Printed in U.S.A.

**Millie Adams** has always loved books. She considers herself a mix of Anne Shirley (loquacious but charming and willing to break a slate over a boy's head if need be) and Charlotte Doyle (a lady at heart but with the spirit to become a mutineer should the occasion arise). Millie lives in a small house on the edge of the woods, which she finds allows her to escape in the way she loves best— in the pages of a book. She loves intense alpha heroes and the women who dare to go toe-to-toe with them (or break a slate over their heads).

### Books by Millie Adams

### Harlequin Presents

*His Secretly Pregnant Cinderella*
*The Billionaire's Baby Negotiation*
*A Vow to Set the Virgin Free*

### *From Destitute to Diamonds*

*The Billionaire's Accidental Legacy*

### *The Kings of California*

*The Scandal Behind the Italian's Wedding*
*Stealing the Promised Princess*
*Crowning His Innocent Assistant*
*The Only King to Claim Her*

Visit the Author Profile page
at Harlequin.com for more titles.

This book is dedicated to my love of all things Christmas. May the magic and joy of the season light you up like a Christmas tree.

# CHAPTER ONE

"AND SHE LIVED happily ever after."

Maren grinned as she headed up the stairs to the glorious palace she now called her home. She was beside herself with the joy of this moment.

Yes. This truly was remarkable.

Every room was perfectly set up to her satisfaction. She peeked in each and every door on her way to her bedroom.

And then she pushed open the door.

Two things registered for her once. The first was that the bed was very large and very pink, and was in fact exactly the bed that she had specified to be put in her room. The bed that she had always dreamed of.

A princess bed.

To go with a princess castle.

The second was that there was a *man* on it.

*Lounging.*

He was—she could see even though he was lying down—very tall. And he was wearing a black suit, and his black hair was pushed off of his forehead in a devilish fashion.

His eyes were black and far too sharp. And she knew beyond a shadow of a doubt that she would remember this moment, and this image, with startling clarity forever.

There was something intense that radiated from him.

Something she could feel, burning deep within her chest, but not something that she could name.

She froze.

It was like looking at a predator. A small voice inside of her whispered run.

But another voice, just as compelling, whispered stay.

So she did, immobile. Inert. When she'd flown in on the helicopter this morning everything had finally made sense.

This? This didn't.

She hadn't known quite what to expect but it wasn't this. Nothing that had happened up till now had prepared her for this.

"Hello, Princess," he said, his voice a silken thread that wound itself around her.

Or perhaps a silken threat.

One letter made quite a lot of difference in this instance, and yet she was far too beset to tell the difference.

"Hello… Hello."

She was acutely aware, just then, of how isolated she was. She'd been feeling isolated in an emotional sense already, but not…cut off.

There were many members of staff in the palace, all around them. Iliana, the household manager, was lovely, and she knew if she screamed people would come running.

And still. In this moment she could hear nothing but her heartbeat.

There was no land to speak of around the palace. It was set entirely on a craggy rock in the Aegean. Golden spires glistened in the sunlight, stretching up toward the sky.

It was the princess palace of her dreams. Resembling strongly both the castle her mother had given her as a child, and the place in her mind where she kept all of her memories.

Her mind palace.

Her sister, Jessie, also in possession of an eidetic memory, thought that the mind palace was fanciful.

Maren didn't see the point of being in charge of the creation of such a thing and having it not be fanciful.

Jessie had told her once that she kept all of her memories in file cabinets.

Maren thought that it was a waste of a brilliant mind.

With all of the details that they stored in their brains, all of the bright and brilliant images they had conjured up over the years, why would you put your memories in anything you could dream up—anything!—a unicorn stable, a fairy house, an enchanted suitcase that opened up to reveal a magical world—into…an office building.

Maren had always dreamed of castles. She'd always believed, hoped, dreamed, that she was meant for something more. Something better. Her mother had sat her down in front of her lighted vanity and let her try on makeup and fix her hair. They'd had the same red hair.

And she'd sang to her. Told her that she was a princess. That she was special.

When her mother went away, that had all gone away.

She'd had a privileged upbringing. Sort of. Growing up, they'd had money, Maren supposed.

Well, their father had. Because he had been a crime lord. They'd had shelter and they'd had food, but none of it had been about their comfort or what they liked, not with Marcus Hargreave. He'd been a monster.

He was dead now. Killed by gunfire exchanged with police when they'd tried to arrest him.

It was for the best.

Her sister, Jessie had a husband and a baby on the way. A girl, who would be Maren's little niece.

She loved the possibility of that future. And it would kill her to think that the baby might be in danger.

Yes, it was all for the best that their father was gone and couldn't hurt anyone ever again. She didn't care about her father.

He had been a horrible man. He had used his daughters to help run his criminal empire. Their minds had been a valuable tool for him.

Maren and Jessie both remembered everything that they saw. Everything. Down to the most minute detail. Jessie was especially good with numbers. Facts.

Maren was good with feelings. The expressions that people made, and the ones that they tried not to.

She was… Well, if she were feeling fanciful—and she often was—she would call herself an empath.

People's feelings seemed to radiate from them and into her.

Right now, his were moving through her like a velvet wave. Dark. Triumphant.

Sensual.

It was unnerving, but then, how could it not be?

She wasn't afraid of him. He was a dangerous man, or rather he could be. There were fractured, complicated emotions in him, she could practically taste them. But he wasn't cruel. Cruelty was an acidic tang on the tongue. Cruelty was what she'd sensed, felt, tasted, every day when near her father and any man who associated with him.

She knew cruel men. He wasn't one of them.

It was not strength, anger, or even an edge of darkness that made a man dangerous. It was whether or not he enjoyed the pain of others.

She knew instantly he did not, and in her life the difference between safety and danger depended on her ability to read people and to trust that reading.

He stood then. She had been correct. He was very, very tall. Broad-shouldered and well-muscled. His movement fluid, like a panther's. That impression only added to that disquiet/excitement rolling through her. The urge to run and the urge to stay.

"I trust that you found everything in the palace to your satisfaction?"

"Well, yes. So far. But…"

"Good. Have you been given a tour of the rooms and grounds?"

"I…"

She had been. As the helicopter she'd been in had descended toward the palace she'd been awed. But even more so when she'd seen it all up close.

The glorious palace itself was made of quartz.

That was why it shone so brightly. That was why it caught the sun in such a brilliant fashion.

The towers were capped in gold.

She'd wondered if they were real gold. Pure gold.

The windows looked like they were made of candy, all brilliant and colorful.

It was quite simply the most beautiful thing she had ever seen in her life, and photographs of it hadn't done it justice. Hadn't begun to show the utter brilliance of what had awaited her.

And the joy she felt…that she and Jessie had done it. That with that last poker game, that very last con, they had escaped their father's legacy, and they had made something for themselves, was overwhelming.

And if Maren felt slightly…undone by the fact that Jessie had found a family through all of this, while Maren had been further isolated, she wouldn't show it.

They'd both been affected by the loss of their mother, of course. Their dearly departed mother, as they sometimes called her.

Though she wasn't dead. She'd just departed.

But it had been her and Jessie against the world for so long. And now it was Jessie, and Ewan and their baby on the way.

She felt like a palace out in the middle of the sea.

Alone. Isolated.

*Gleaming*, though.

A *princess*, though.

She'd had to wait months to claim her own poker prize. And the timing was good. Because Jessie and Ewan should have some time to themselves and they didn't need a lonely relation wafting around.

So now here she was. Ready to grasp what was hers.

But she had not just won the palace. She had won

the royal seat of what was its own principality out here in the middle of the water.

She was a princess now.

Princess Maren.

She had always known that she was destined to be a princess.

*Of course you're a princess, Maren.*

The strong memory of her mother's voice, of her smiling at her, warmed Maren.

*The most beautiful princess there is. And a princess ought to have jewels.*

Her mother had loved to let Maren try on her jewels. Her dresses.

Her mother had been the most beautiful woman in the world. But she had been married to an ogre of a man.

And she'd had to leave.

Maren understood. She supposed.

Though it didn't mean that she didn't miss her mother terribly. Every day.

She brought her mind firmly back to the present.

It was both a blessing and a curse that she could remember those times with her mother with perfect, never fading clarity.

Sometimes, if she sat alone in a room, and went to that palace in her mind, it was like having a visit with her mother. Nothing new could happen, of course. But it was nice to remember.

It was nice.

And when she'd dreamed, she'd dreamed of a palace of her own…

And a child to share it with.

She couldn't have her mother back, but she could make a family of her own. Give all that love she had inside of her. She could *be* the best mother.

Jessie had gotten pregnant and hadn't even been sure she'd wanted a baby. That had made Maren feel slightly… It had hurt, was all.

She *wanted* a baby. She had for a long time. Her sister had gone and gotten pregnant on accident and it had been a huge drama for her. Which was fair. Jessie was different than Maren. But it had still made her feel a bit wounded.

She was closer now, though. To the life she wanted. The life she needed.

Sure, it had been accomplished through gambling. Which in any way she was philosophically opposed to, but she was also predisposed to being very, very good at it. And she had to embrace the idea of making a future for themselves using the resources that they had.

Plus, a fool and his money were soon parted.

It was not *her* fault that the men that sat down at poker tables with her had been fools.

And the old man that she had won the castle from had been very much a fool indeed.

He'd been raving about how if he lost it—and he'd

been certain he wouldn't—it would at least keep that madman from…

A strange, cold sensation gripped her.

"Who… Who are you?"

But she had a feeling she might know.

She had a feeling this might be the madman.

The curve of his mouth did little to convince her otherwise.

"My name is Acastus Diakos. And I am your husband."

# CHAPTER TWO

SHE WAS A VISION.

He could not quite believe his good fortune. Not that it mattered whether or not the Princess of the Palace on the Rock was beautiful or not. The woman could look like chewed-up leather and he would still be obligated to create an heir with her.

The terms of his family promise would be fulfilled.

He would give no quarter on this.

They had waited, all his life they had waited, for the Argos family to give them their due. And then Stavros Argos had given the Palace on the Rock away, and along with it had transferred his promise.

But that she was lovely…it was a nice surprise.

She was looking at him, shocked. "I… That… That makes no sense."

"Don't tell me you failed to read the fine print on the agreement that you signed."

"I didn't." She frowned. "It wasn't on the agreement I signed!"

"Princess, you should have received an almanac with all of this information. It was an addendum to your paperwork."

"I... I didn't though!"

He did know that. He'd intercepted the almanac. He hadn't needed her backing out of the agreement when it was important—essential—that the terms were fulfilled.

Stavros had been so against Acastus marrying his daughter that he'd gambled the palace away rather than see his promises fulfilled. Rather than see their bloodlines mix. He'd sought to undo the vows made between the families and to deny his family the honor they'd been promised.

The honor they deserved.

He'd worked in this palace as a boy. Scrubbed floors while Stavros put a boot on his back, and he'd done it because his father had commanded it. Because he had said they were earning their right to be royalty.

Stavros thought he was winning by passing the palace off, but in fact it was a total victory for the Diakos clan. Argos would be erased from the line at this moment, and Diakos would be the name that carried on.

The palace of myth and legend and story would finally belong to his family. They would be kings and queens. And his children would always bear the title they'd been promised, they would not clean floors. They would not debase themselves for a man who was just one in a long line of men who had made promises and broken them.

Acastus had vowed he would see this through to completion.

And Acastus kept his word.

"We are married," he said. "By taking up the throne you have taken a husband."

"But I thought that meant being a princess. And wearing a dress. I didn't say any *vows*."

"They were built into the contract."

"That can't be legal."

"This rock we are on is its own sovereign nation, as you know. It is not only legal, it is binding."

She blinked. "If I step off the rock, are we not married then?"

"No."

She looked around the room.

"What?"

"I'm looking for a hidden camera," she said. "I was starting to wonder if I was being pranked."

She was even beautiful when she was incredulous. "Sadly no. The Diakos family has been owed their place in the royal line for generations. We served the Palace on the Rock for five hundred years. In a great battle, all those years ago, an Argos saved a Diakos on the field of battle, and we swore allegiance. And we have been promised a place in the lineage for at least as long. And now time is up."

"It seems rather arbitrary."

"It isn't. I promise you. It is the law. As binding as your own agreement was, I have one of my own. An agreement forged in the blood of generations."

She wrinkled her nose. "Couldn't they have used ink?"

She did not fear him, this girl. It was a good thing, he supposed. If they were to make a child she could not fear him. But Acastus had never been...

*Personable.*

He was a ruthless businessman, brilliant in all things, in possession of a keen mind and not even a hint of modesty.

He had influence and power, he had no need of modesty or an engaging personality. Women found him sexy because he was remote. Who was he to question it?

He examined the expression on Maren's face. She did not seem to find him sexy so much as infuriating, but she would need time.

He'd known he was surprising her with the marriage. A gamble. But she'd gambled to win this place and he'd decided to take his chances as well.

"What does it mean... Does Iliana know that you're here?"

"Of course," he said. "She was well aware of the marriage agreement."

"I was not."

"A shame. It would've been nice if you would've been prepared."

"Well, don't go making it sound like that. That I somehow *shirked* my duties. Nobody *told* me. I did not get the almanac which apparently explained the 'duties' I was agreeing to."

"You signed papers."

"None of this makes any sense. I won the castle from a very old Greek man…"

"Yes. I know who you won the castle from. Stavros Argos. He did not wish for me to touch his daughter, and in fact, was so against my ever touching her, he was willing to lose the Palace on the Rock, his family legacy, to ensure I did not. He sought to end the obligation his family had to mine, he sought to ensure my family did not win, and yet, he did not count on me."

"On you doing what?"

"Coming here and fulfilling the terms of the marriage bargain. He thought I cared about marrying an Argos. I don't. I care about my legacy. I care about the titles. I care about what is owed."

She frowned. "Why…why would he do that? Why make the agreement if he wanted out of it?"

"This agreement is much older than we are."

"Well…why…" She cleared her throat. "You seem like a very nice man." She wrinkled her nose. "A nice man?" He glared at her. "A man. And a very tall one. So why is he so opposed to you marrying his daughter? I don't suppose it has anything to do with what she wants. He didn't seem like a man who would care about that at all."

"Oh, he doesn't. He's making me pay." He smiled. "He's a fool. He thought I wanted his daughter. I don't."

"She's well rid of you, isn't she?"

He laughed. It was funny, at least he thought that was what he felt. He so rarely found anything funny it was hard to say. "Yes. Undoubtedly."

"Woe unto me then."

"I suppose that all depends." He regarded her closely.

She looked quite alarmed. He almost would've felt sorry for her if he'd possessed that level of feeling.

But he was cold. Through and through.

Life had made Acastus that way. He had to be that way.

If he did not claim this now, the suffering of their generations would mean nothing.

The suffering he and his mother had endured would mean nothing.

And that meant, that it had to be seen through.

"So he gave the castle to *me*, a stranger, to avoid you?"

"Yes. He's a fool. He surrendered all to try and hurt me—he did not think it through."

"Well. He lost. He may not have planned to lose."

She shook her coppery hair. "In my experience, men, particularly of a certain age, don't think I can beat them. They're invariably wrong."

He shrugged. "He did lose, whether he planned to or not. The legacy he lost for his daughter in his petty spite. Though Elena Argos has no great fondness for this place. I do not believe she wishes to leave her glamorous life abroad for a position here in the sea."

"In fairness, if I had a glamorous life in Paris I'm not sure I would have left it either."

"What a fool. And now the title will belong to me, belong to my children, my family will gain access to the royal line, through marriage."

She shrunk back. "That's quite archaic. My title doesn't even mean anything."

He lifted a brow. "Then surrender it."

"Absolutely *not*," she said, holding her hands to her breast as if she was clutching some imaginary thing. "It's *mine*."

She was like him. She wanted this.

Which was what he'd hoped. What he'd needed.

"Yes. And it doesn't work that way. You have married me by signing the papers and this cannot be undone. And we are to have a child."

Her cheeks went scarlet, like an innocent, and he felt his body respond. "I don't even *know* you," she said.

"You will know me soon enough."

Then she did something he did not expect. She

threw her hands in the air and shrieked, and stomped. As she paced back and forth in the bedroom.

"This is unreasonable! I am a princess! How do I have less control now than I did before?"

"That is a hallmark of royal life, I'm afraid," he said, deliberately keeping his voice monotone to irritate her.

"I don't like it!" She stamped again for good measure.

He recalled a story he'd read as a child, *The Butterfly who Stamped*. She reminded him of that. All soft and fluttery, and then acute and sharp in her outrage.

She was emotional, this woman. The world would not be kind to her. Unless she stayed here, shut away, and she would have the luxury of doing so if she wished. He required little of her.

And then she leveled her gaze at him. "You did it, didn't you?"

"I did what?"

"You made sure I didn't get the almanac. So I wouldn't know. So I would sign everything and come here."

"Did I?" he asked, feigning innocence.

"Oh, Acastus Diakos. Don't try to con a con artist. You'll only embarrass yourself. I'm an expert at manipulation myself. You seem like a novice."

"And yet. Here you are, married to me."

She sniffed. "It isn't an elegant con."

"I'm all right with being perceived as ham-fisted if that means I win."

"Ooh!" She let out a sound halfway between a growl and a howl. "You are infuriating."

"And you're still here."

"Well, it's my castle."

"Fantastic. Then you are my wife."

She was so soft looking.

She was wearing a pale pink gown, her gingery red hair falling in a silken curtain around her face.

She had a smattering of freckles across her nose, and her green eyes tilted up at the outside corners.

Her pale pink lips were extraordinary. Her upper lip fuller than the one on the bottom.

He had not been with a woman in some time.

And he felt that now. Every night of his celibacy.

He was too involved in his work. That was the problem.

He had been taxing himself to get everything in order to make sure that all of his luxury hotel brands could run themselves effectively while he saw to his business here for the next month.

He would not remain on the island. Functionally, taking Maren as a wife would hardly change anything.

Having a child would hardly change anything.

All of it was symbolic.

But since his life had been filled with suffering

that was more symbolic than he would like, he had decided that the symbolism mattered.

"The thing is," she said, walking toward him, her finger extended. "You're crazy. And nobody gets married for these sorts of reasons."

"You're incorrect. Royalty gets married for these sorts of reasons all the time. It is dynastic. And dynasty is what matters. My family is an ancient one. Our name is one filled with great pride. My father lived on the edge of a sheep farm for all of his days. He would take us by boat to the palace and we would work. Clean. He kept us in poverty. He kept us beneath the boot of the Argos family. He promised my mother she would be royal, and he failed her. He did nothing but wait. Wait for the promise to be fulfilled."

She shrugged. "I don't know what to tell you, this came with some money, but not an astronomical amount. Really, the value is in the property. In the title. I do like being a princess. But I'm bringing my own fortune, and I'm certainly not giving—"

He laughed. For the second time. It nearly startled him. It was so foreign, that sound, coming out of his mouth. Dark and not filled with humor the way that it might be if another person were to make the sound. But then, he himself was not filled with humor.

"I do not need your money. My *father* lived in poverty for all of his life. I did not. I'm a billionaire several times over, Ms. Hargreave. I've no need for money."

"Then why are you here?"

His life was a wasteland of broken promises and the pain they'd caused. The failures of his father. This was what his mother had wanted, what he'd worked so hard for—all for her. She'd wanted this title. She wanted to know the next generation was secured. Or rather, she wanted a grandchild. And he was willing to provide that, both for her and the legacy.

For all the work, all the suffering, it could not be only him who saw this palace in the Diakos name, finally. It had to be his children, and his children's children, and on down the line until they'd had their five hundred years restored and then some.

Life itself was fleeting. A legacy was what mattered.

His father's legacy was disappointment. Broken promises to the woman he'd married, and to the child he'd begotten.

Acastus's would be victory.

"I told you. I will have a royal heir. I will have a title. We will see the promises honored. A fulfillment of the sacrifice that they made. My great-uncle died fighting a war on behalf of the royal family. And before that, there were others. Lost children. Dead husbands. Sent into every conflict that the royal family of the Palace on the Rock deemed appropriate for them to fight in."

"Oh, I don't think we will be doing wars," Maren said, frowning. "I don't like them."

"I will be repaid," he said, intensity making his throat seize tight. "We will have recompense."

She took a step back. "I just think… I think that it seems a bit… It's a bit unorthodox."

"Indeed it is. But you're not in a position to negotiate. You signed yourself away."

She angled her head and squinted. "Did I *really*?"

"You did. The almanac you're looking for is under your pillow, Princess. Like a pea."

"That was under mattresses."

"Go ahead. Be off with you and look at what all that you have signed entails. The history of the country is there for all the world to see. Look at the marital promise between the Argus family and the Diakos family. Tell me what you find."

He straightened his black tie and walked to the door of the bedroom. "My chambers are down the hall. I will see you at dinner."

"I… What if I don't want a dinner guest?"

"That is no way to treat your husband," he responded.

"I have not decided if you are my husband."

"I already am. It is both simple and unambiguous. I will see you at dinner."

And then he turned and left her standing there, a

sense of triumph beating in his breast as he walked down the corridor.

Finally, this place would be his. Finally, there would be restitution for all that had been lost.

He would uphold the promise made to his ancestors.

The promise he'd made to his mother. His mother had married his father on the understanding that she would someday be Queen Mother, an honorary title that would be given when Acastus married the Princess of the Palace on the Rock. That they would be wealthy, and all their needs met. That they wouldn't labor, but have people serving them.

What Acastus saw as the real failure on his father's part, was how he had poured everything into being obsequious to Stavros, and had not supported them. They'd been hand-to-mouth, always. Working in the palace and going home to a hovel.

Why had he not sought to better them at all? Why had he put everything into that future promise? That future marriage?

Acastus had not done so. Acastus had not rested. He'd picked up this burden, and every other, and had carried them up the hill to this moment.

Victory was finally at hand.

# CHAPTER THREE

MAREN SPENT THE next hour reading the almanac. The bastard. He'd deliberately withheld this from her, she knew it. But she and Jessie had manipulated the world as con artists for years. It would be…dishonest for her to act shocked or wounded by this. What you put out in the world was what you got back.

This, she supposed, was her con woman karma. Complete with a castle and a husband.

Ascending the throne had seemed like a lark when she'd first won. It had been made out to be such a small nation when it had been presented to her. It had seemed rather…*inconsequential* that it was a country. The royalty part had seemed like such a formality that she hadn't even considered that there might be a secret marriage law bound up in all of it.

But indeed. She was now a full and complete expert on the history between the two families. Hundreds of years ago the Diakos family swore fealty to the Argos royals, and they in turn promised that at the end of a period of servitude, they would be grafted into the family through marriage. An eligible son marrying an eligible daughter, or a Diakos daughter to an Argos son.

But why? she wondered.

Why had the Diakos family served the Argos family like this? Especially when they had spent generations failing to live up to their promises.

There had been many Argos daughters that could've married Diakos sons, or in reverse. But they had not been given in marriage.

And on and on it went.

She wasn't an Argos. But still, she could see that it had passed to "the royal family of the Palace on the Rock."

She was a royal family of one.

But why not just give the title to…a man whose name sounded like a sneeze.

*Acastus Diakos.*

What sort of nonsense was that?

She looked into the room that had all of her finery in it, and her jaw dropped.

The room was well lit, with gowns on displays as if they were in a boutique. On mannequins, on lighted platforms, bags and hats elevated on shelves. Floor to ceiling glamour everywhere she looked.

Her mother would have loved this.

The thought made her stomach go tight.

She knew that it wasn't technically a formal dinner, but she decided to put on a pink, frothy gown that was fashioned from a spray of netting. It was so delightfully over-the-top and feminine and she'd always found a certain amount of power in such things.

When she and Jessie played poker they counted on a hyper-feminine appearance, on their beauty, to make men underestimate them.

She put gold makeup on her face, delighting in the items that she found in the glorious bathroom suite.

And when she went downstairs, she did her best to smile and look serene.

Because she was not going to allow this man to think that he had shaken her.

Even though she felt well and thoroughly shaken.

But she'd been in worse situations than this. She'd flirted and smiled and cajoled information out of random men countless times with her hair styled into bouncy curls and a dress that swirled around the tops of her thighs. Looking as sweet and vulnerable as possible, while being aware of every item around her she could use as a weapon if need be.

She'd grown up with a narcissistic sociopath for a father. She had learned how to protect herself, just in case. She didn't walk through life afraid because she was prepared. She paid attention to details. She was always alert.

She only looked soft.

Her mother had been soft, and so desperately in

love with their father. And his betrayal of her had been so unendurable she'd had to leave.

He was a narcissistic sociopath.

Maren understood why a woman couldn't stay with a narcissistic sociopath.

Maren wasn't as naïve as her mother had been when she'd married Maren's father, because she'd been raised not to be.

She wouldn't be naïve now.

When she walked in, he was already seated there, at the head of the table, lounging.

Did the man do nothing but lounge?

"I have a question for you," she said as she walked in.

"Yes?"

"First of all, what is it you do."

He lifted a brow, the arrogant set of his jaw somehow intensifying even as he barely moved. "Do you not know who I am?"

And suddenly…she matched his face to images she'd seen before.

She felt her eyes pop wide. "Acastus Diakos? The billionaire real estate developer who routinely tops the lists of youngest self-made billionaires?"

"Oh, so you've read the write-ups."

"I've seen them. On newsstands. I can't forget things. It's sort of a quirk."

He frowned. "What sort of quirk?"

"An *actual condition* sort of quirk. When I say I

remember everything, I mean I could recite the almanac back to you now."

"All of it?"

She sighed. "Here in this book, and in accordance with…"

"That's fine," he said, holding up a hand.

"So yes, I know who you are. Though I'm not sure you should be flattered by it. It's just a little hat trick I do."

He laughed. It was the same dark laugh she'd heard twice in her room, and it was…odd. It was not filled with humor. It made her feel cold.

She could read feelings easily, she could feel them. Taste them. Gauge their temperature. His were contrasts, and she found them strange. His laugh was a shard of ice. There was no humor in it. It sounded rich to the ear, but the quality of it…it was flat and sharp and the taste was acidic.

"It seems to me it's a card trick you do," he said. "Is that how you won the game?"

"Yes," she said, without hesitation. "I know it's frowned on but I can't help how my brain works. It's not intentional cheating, I don't have aces up my sleeve."

"And yet, I think if the men who lost to you knew…"

She batted her eyelashes. "How would they know? They'd have to admit that I might be smarter than they are, and I think we both know that would never happen."

He regarded her closely and she had the feeling of being a small butterfly, pinned down to a board. "What you're telling me is that I am to underestimate you at my peril?"

She nodded. "I suppose so. Though if you want to underestimate me, I won't stop you." She looked around the massive room. Her dining room, let it not be forgotten. This man might have installed himself here, but it was not his.

She looked down, and then back up, fixing him with her most intense gaze, which she'd been told before was quite unnerving. "Why do you think that this settles the score between yourself and the Argos family? I am not an Argos."

"You are not. But that isn't the point, the point is that I am after the title, the legacy, the Argos family means nothing to me, and he was narcissistic enough to imagine that being enmeshed in his disgraceful family was what I was after. He sought to deny me, but I am not denied."

"Why did he care so much? Why does he hate you?"

"It is…complicated."

She laughed, she couldn't help it. Her laugh was not flat, sharp or confusing. "Oh, come now. Humans are never complicated. Power, money or sex?"

"What?"

"Is the issue related to power, money or sex? I find it almost always is."

"You are wrong. Ego." He did not elaborate.

"Go on," she said.

"I see no reason to go on. The fact is, this is the only way. My father was an ineffective man. A man who was not brave enough to seize a life for his family. He was content to wait. I will not wait."

"I can understand the difficult father part."

"Tell me about your father," he said.

"Not yet," she said, feeling a pang of distaste at the idea of having to think about her father, and her life growing up in his criminal compound. "I want to talk more about this. Practically, what do you hope to achieve by having…a marriage into this…royal family of one. As I pointed out to you before, it isn't like I'm actually a member of the Argos family. How is that a legacy?"

"It doesn't matter. It is a matter of the history books. Of what will be written."

"Great. Does anybody write about principalities that don't have anyone living in them?"

"My family sacrificed and bled and gave for generations. Not for nothing. It will not be undone."

"And it's worth marrying a stranger for?" Maren had never given a lot of thought to marriage. She'd never thought she'd marry, and here she was.

She had loved Jessie's wedding. It had been so beautiful and romantic.

"It will not be a typical marriage," he said. "I have no designs on having a wife. Not in a real sense. We shall not share bedrooms or speak to each other over orange juice and toast in the mornings. I wish to marry into the family. I wish to have all the benefits of that marriage. And we shall have a child."

She felt her face got hot. "The thing is, a lot of people would argue that if we are going to have a baby, that would be a real..." She blinked. "Oh. Of course. We could do IVF."

"We cannot."

"Why not?"

"Maren," he said, his voice low and cajoling, as if he was speaking to a child. She didn't like it.

She frowned. "Don't talk to me like I'm a child. I'm not a child. I'm just not well-versed in this particular level of strangeness that I seem to have found myself enmeshed in."

"You have heard, I suppose, that there is no such thing as a free lunch?"

"Yes."

"But you thought there was such a thing as a free castle?"

"It wasn't *free*. I won it. Fair and square." Well. That was overstating it. She had won it via counting cards and having an especially good ability to read the faces of those around her. But, it wasn't her fault that she could just do those things naturally. It wasn't like she had cards up her sleeve, now that really would've been cheating. She and Jessie cheated, sort of. It was just using natural methods.

"Fair and square," he said. "Okay then. Do you really think that things this big come this easily? Did you really think that a building this old, containing this many ghosts, would be given to you and you would suffer none of the echoes of the past? This is foolishness."

"It's foolishness to not realize that there was going to be a husband waiting for me in my bedroom. Also, why couldn't we do IVF?"

"You don't seem averse to the idea of having a baby."

"I'm not," she said.

If she was being objective the man in front of her was an absolute pillar of masculinity. He was well over six feet tall, broad-shouldered, his bone structure was stunning. Quite possibly, he was the most beautiful man she had ever seen in her life. If she was going to give genetic material to a child, she could certainly do worse. Shame about his personality, but as they were still on the fence about nature versus nurture, she was pretty sure that she could still work with it. He said that he didn't want a real marriage, fine. She didn't want to have orange juice and toast with him either. And there was no reason they couldn't...

"It is stipulated in the marriage contract that in

order for a child to count as an heir they must be conceived *ek fyeseos*."

"What?"

"By nature."

Maren nearly choked. "I'm sorry, what?"

"This was an old way of defining that they could not bring in a child that was not of their genetic material."

She couldn't believe what she was hearing. "That is *highly* offensive."

He lifted a dark brow. "It may shock you to learn the ancient peoples were not concerned with the offense of modern peoples."

"It's extremely offensive to adopted—"

He held up a hand. "Maren, no one cares. These are the rules. The stipulations. And it would be argued now, I believe, that any sort of unnatural method of conception would not fall under the parameters."

"This just seems very *medieval*."

He waved his hand as if to dismiss her concern. "It's a castle. Of course it's medieval."

Maren felt just slightly like hissing and spitting. He was so condescending. And he was suggesting… Well, what he was suggesting didn't even bear thinking about.

"I don't even know you."

"What does that have to do with anything?"

She regarded him for a long moment. And as she

did so, two feelings, one familiar, and one disconcertingly unfamiliar, wound through her.

He was beautiful. There was no denying that. The
impact of him was stunning, and it was a testament
to that beauty the degree to which she could find
herself immobilized by it even as she faced these
extraordinary circumstances. The other feeling was
a frightening familiarity. The sensation of looking
at a man whose feelings were so buried, so remote,
that she could not read them.

Her father had been like that. A man of inscruta-
ble cruelty, who had seemed to make decisions about
what he was doing without real thought. He simply
acted. Simply did whatever seemed right and best.
There was no emotional baseline that it seemed to
come from. It just was.

He felt like that. Like something remote and far
away.

But the mix of it with that bright burn… That was
what frightened her.

Well, that and the fact he was standing there
calmly suggesting that they conceive a baby.

She had never even been kissed.

She tried to imagine it. Tried to imagine this wild,
unreadable creature moving to her. Lowering his
head and claiming her mouth.

She liked romance novels. She liked romance. In
theory. She had long believed that she might be able
to put off some of her own romantic longings by con-

suming media that depicted love and sex. She had such a vivid imagination.

She had spent many long nights lying awake imagining a man trailing his large hands over her body. Kissing her. Possessing her. And even more importantly than that, holding her. Treating her like she was something special. Something precious.

He would not hold her like that.

But she knew that he would touch her.

His hands… She wondered if they would be expert.

He was gorgeous, glorious. She imagined that they would be.

That they would be skilled and knowing. That he could teach her things about her body, about lust that would set her on fire.

But did she want that?

Because that was the problem with a memory like hers.

The images didn't fade. The feelings. It was all disconcertingly present all the time.

Those moments with her mother, a blessing and a curse.

The fear of living under her father's thumb.

It was why when she and Jessie had run away Maren had made very strict rules for them.

She had been worried especially about Jessie, who had a wildness and a sharpness about her that Maren simply didn't possess.

Maren had always been soft.

She had always known that she could be easily broken. That if she loved and the person didn't love her in return, it would destroy her.

That she would always be left wanting more. Worried that it wasn't enough.

That she could never be enough.

If she slept with a man and he gave her brilliant pleasure, the memory of that pleasure would never go away.

*He's your husband.*

But what did that even mean?

"Here's the problem," she said. "The way that I see it. How do I know I won't fall in love with you?"

He stared at her. She supposed she should be embarrassed to ask the question, but she wasn't. Because it wasn't as if she was on the verge of falling in love with him or anything. It was a pure hypothetical. "It's a very serious issue," she said. "From what I've been told virgins often equate sex and love."

"You're a virgin?" he asked.

"Yes," she said. "I've had a very irregular life. I have a very irregular brain. I have to worry about things that other people don't have to worry about. My memories once impressed into my mind do not go away. Not ever. They're always there. As vivid as they were the day they occurred. So you tell me, why would I give myself an endless stream of sexual images that I can't escape? I suppose some people might want that. But I never did. And I've always been very cautious. And here I find myself confronted by a very handsome man who thinks he can just sweep in and demand access to my body."

"You will forgive me. I did not anticipate that you had never…"

"You made assumptions. You know what they say about assumptions."

"I don't."

She was satisfied that she got to say it. "They make an ass out of you and me. So in this case only *you*. I'm not an ass. I didn't cause this issue."

"You didn't read the almanac," he pointed out.

She planted her hands on the table and stood abruptly. "I never got it," she shouted. "I never got it, and you acting like I was irresponsible in some way is outrageous. I didn't create this situation. You're the one that's bound and determined to take the title. Why do you even need a baby?"

She felt annoyed with herself for getting so angry. It reminded her of bad times growing up in her father's house. It reminded her of the explosions between her parents that had eventually made it so her mother went away.

"It's heritage. Lineage. It is about ensuring that the future of my family is greater than its past."

"Philosophical for *you*. It is personal to me. I would like a baby. That's the thing. That is the reason that I haven't stabbed you."

"Stabbed me?"

"Have you paid attention to nothing that I've said? I had a very irregular life. My sister and I…" She supposed this was the part where she had to talk about her father. "My father is a madman. Flat-out. Well, he was. He's dead now. But that's the problem. It's the *memories*. He feels like he's right here with me even when he isn't. I think of him, and I can see everything that he ever did. He was a criminal warlord kind of guy. And when my sister and I ran away from him, when we refused to continue to be tools in his arsenal, we had to live in fear. We tried to protect ourselves at all costs. So yeah. If I had to stab you, I would. But the only reason that I'm sitting here listening to this is that I'm tired of being alone."

He didn't look shocked, or even all that aggrieved by her revelation about her father, and she wasn't quite sure what to do with that.

"You have mistaken me," he said. "I don't actually need a running commentary on your thought process. What I would like to know is if we are at an impasse or not. If you don't agree to this, I will challenge your ownership of the castle. So it's entirely up to you. What's more important. Your virginity, or being a princess?"

"Being a princess, obviously. I didn't expect to keep my virginity for my whole life. I was just being cautious about it." It was amazing how easy that answer was. But it made her heart beat faster. Just then, the waiter came in holding pizza entrées.

The food was set down in front of them and he looked at her, somewhat surprised. "Pizza?"

"Yes," she said. "It's what I wanted. I'm the Princess. So I asked for pizza."

He reached out and took a slice and she found even that movement was predatory. She'd have hoped that him swooping in for a slice of pizza might transform him into a more manageable creature. Something almost human. Alas.

"You would rather have a baby with me than remain a virgin?" he asked.

And she did her very best not to imagine it. Thankfully, she'd never done it before so while she knew all about sex in theory, the images of it didn't loom as clear as images of that which she'd experienced.

"Yes," she said. "But we will need to come to a very strict set of rules."

"And those are?"

She took a bite of her pizza and spoke around it. She was amused by the distaste on his face. "Sex for conception only."

"And what does that mean?"

"We will wait until I am at my most fertile, and then you can… Do your best."

He lifted a brow, and pressed his hands to his forehead. "My best."

"Well, yes." She chewed her pizza thoughtfully. "I don't want you to get performance anxiety. I hear men are very touchy that way."

His expression was extremely flat. "I shall do my best."

"It's all we can ask of you."

He looked at her, hard, and she had to wonder if she was really on the verge of agreeing to this. Hell, she supposed she already had.

But she had wanted a whole new life.

What he was offering didn't conflict with anything. And it gave her one thing she wanted. That she wanted desperately. A child.

And that mattered to her. It mattered so much.

"What are your terms?"

"Beyond the conception thing? You said that you don't want much to do with the child."

"I would like the child to know that they have a father. A father who works to provide for them. I am a billionaire. As you pointed out this palace has not come with an exceptional store of wealth. However, you will have access to that wealth through me."

"Oh," she said, feeling dizzy. "I have access to it?"

"Yes," he said. "You do. You are my wife, and I will take care of my wife."

"What else?"

"My mother will be in residence here sometimes. She always dreamed of it. I will be here when she is here. And she will be considered part of the royal line."

"Sure. That's fine."

She didn't see why the titles couldn't get spread around. Everyone ought to get some enjoyment out of them.

"But as for being with one another day in and day out... I've no desire for that."

"And as far as... As I said, I don't want to go falling in love with you. You do not seem like the sort of man who could love."

She didn't need the drama that might come with them trying to cohabitate. It made tension creep up her spine to think of it. It made her think too much of her parents.

Something sharpened in his gaze. "And why do you think that?"

"You're cold. I can feel it. It's the way that you are. It's a strange sort of contrast, because there is something in you that has a spark. That feels hot, but at the same time you... No. You are not the sort of man that I would wish to pin any dreams on."

"You are smart," he said. "You shouldn't. I will mostly live in Greece. That's where the headquarters for my businesses are. I travel quite a bit. I will engage in affairs as I see fit, of course. I'm a man with a certain voracity of sexual appetite. And if you do not wish for the fulfillment of that appetite to fall to you, then you must accept that while I offer my money, my protection, and my support, I do not offer my fidelity. Neither do I expect it from you."

It was easy enough to see how that would hurt. She would take him into her bed over these next weeks to try and conceive a baby. And then he would be gone. But she would have the expectation. None of it would be a surprise. If she wished to take lovers she could, and she could be in control of that. She had the palace. She had money. She would not be in a desperate position. Those were the sorts of things that created situations that were ripe for heartbreak.

She didn't want to be desperate, she didn't want heartbreak. But she was not desperate anymore, and she didn't love this man. So perhaps this was it. That step toward the life that she truly wanted.

The step toward being a new, self-contained person. Someone who didn't rely on her sister to be her emotional support.

Jessie loved her, but she had to make her own life. Just like her mother had loved her, but had to get away from their father. She understood. She did.

Maren needed to make her own life. When she had a child, she would… She would never leave that child. She would never have to.

*This man is a stranger.*

Yes. And she recognized that coldness in him. But it wasn't the same as her father. There was no cruelty to it.

At the same time, she could see that developing feelings for him would be a fool's errand.

He was a renowned businessman, he was not a criminal. He was… He was as safe as anyone.

"I would like to sign papers. Ensuring that no matter what I will retain custody of our child."

"By all means," he said. "We can certainly do that. As I said, what I'm after is the legacy. And unlike my father, I will not be weak or ineffective."

"You really don't like your father."

"My father is dead," he said. "And when he died, I decided to pick us up and elevate us in the world. My mother spent their entire marriage waiting for him to fulfill promises. While he waited for another man to hand him money. To hand him royalty. I want the promise, but I did not wait to make my mother comfortable. And now she will have the title that she was long promised. She will have no more reason to weep. My father gave her many. From his life debasing himself to his premature death, when all promise of happiness died with him."

"Yes. I relate to that too," she said softly. "My father gave my mother a lot of reasons to weep. Maybe that's one reason I've always been afraid of men. Falling in love with them, anyway. My mother fell in love with the wrong one."

"You are forewarned. Is that not the same as being forearmed? You know that I am not offering love. What I am offering is something better. What I am offering you is security. All of the money to ensure that this castle is run. You can be a princess. And you will have your child."

"It almost seems like there's no downside," she said.

The corner of his mouth tipped upward. "None at all."

"Well, then... Well."

"There is just one thing left to do. We ought to seal our marriage with a kiss."

And before Maren could protest he had risen from his chair, and crossed the space between them. Then he reached out to her, hauled her up and pressed her against the hard inferno that was his body.

Her heart was beating erratically, her body nearly shorting out.

She had been in a lot of different situations.

She had conned men at poker games. And in some of those situations, she had ended up in a bit of physical peril.

Men had tried to steal kisses from her before.

But it had been different. Because she hadn't felt her body respond.

Here and now she did. Here and now, she felt herself leaning toward him. She felt herself wanting.

And that had never happened before.

She did not feel in danger, she felt as if she was standing on the edge of a precipice with beautiful clear water below. Yes, it was dangerous. But all she had to do was allow their mouths to meet, and she would be plunged into something new. Something she had never experienced before.

And then, between a breath and her next heartbeat, he lowered his head, and pressed his mouth to hers.

And she was tossed beneath the waves.

## CHAPTER FOUR

HE HAD NOT counted on this. On her softness.

On her flavor being so rich and intoxicating it overtook him.

He was Acastus Diakos, and he was not a man accustomed to feeling out of his depth. In fact, he had not had that happen since he was a boy.

Since he'd been thrown in the dungeon of this very castle, punished and imprisoned by Stavros Argos.

Since his own father had allowed it to happen. A fitting punishment for his crime, which had been designed to ensure that Acastus never got what was owed him.

This was like that. Disorienting. Like fumbling around in the dark.

He had kissed countless women. There was no reason this one should be different.

She was a stranger, and that in and of itself was not especially different for him.

He was a man who enjoyed a one-night stand.

He did not know his lovers.

But Maren was his wife, a woman he was to conceive a child with.

He had never made love to a woman without a condom. Had never slid inside the warm welcome of the female body without a latex barrier between him and that glorious slick channel. Perhaps it was the thought of that.

And yet it was so base.

He did not consider himself that sort of man.

He had appetites, but he was not a libertine. He was not driven by those things. He was driven by something bigger, he always had been.

It was not about his immediate satisfaction. He was always investing in the future. And this should be about the child. This should be about the triumph of winning.

But it wasn't that which made his body so hard that he ached now. Wasn't that which fired flame through his veins.

It had nothing to do with victory. And everything to do with her.

With the small kitten sounds she made as he forced her lips apart beneath his and slid his tongue against hers.

As he moved his hands down to cup the softness of her rear, and grind his hardness against her.

It was simply need.

Simply desire. Nothing more.

And yet there was nothing simple about it. It was an endless well of longing. Of need.

She was just so soft.

He could get lost in it. In her.

His life was hard. Sharp angles in a fast pace.

And she beckoned him to something different. Something more.

He had thought to use this moment to ensnare her. To ensure that he won. And yet she was the one drawing him in.

She was the one making him ache. Pushing him beyond himself.

She was the one.

Abruptly, he drew away from her. But ceasing contact didn't do anything to help the storm that was raging through him. Her eyes were wide, the color high in her cheeks. Her lips were pink and swollen from his attentions.

She looked like a woman ripe for seduction.

"Oh, my," she said, looking dazed.

She was breathing heavy, her eyes glassy, her lips swollen.

"That was…acceptable," he said, his own voice rough.

She slid her hand up behind his neck, looking at him with wonder. She pushed her fingers through his hair. A crease deepened between her brows as she looked at him. He should pull away and yet he found the concentration she was focusing on him to be intoxicating.

"And you know," she said, her voice a broken whisper. "The problem with that is that I will always remember it. The exact moment that you took me into your arms. The way it felt to have my breasts pressed to your chest. The way it felt when your tongue slid against mine. What is a woman to do with such a thing? To know that always and forever that moment will be burned into my mind?"

He knew without a doubt that it would be burned into his as well. But he rejected the way he felt drawn to her now. The way he felt like he'd die if he didn't touch her.

"We will suit," he said. "That is lucky."

"Is it?" she asked, her voice shaky. "If we aren't going to be together after the conception of the baby... Well then, what does it matter?"

"It matters, because we will be spending the next few days in bed. Will we not?"

"I...suppose so. Though we can make it as perfunctory as we like."

He wanted to laugh at her. Yet he didn't find it funny.

"We shall see. If it's going to be burned into your memory, Maren, ought it not to be a stunning memory?"

"I suppose," she said, capturing one of those swollen lips in her teeth. "I suppose."

"Should you like your pizza?"

"Yes," she said quickly, sitting down in front of her plate. "I'll have to check my tracking app for sure, but I think I'm not fertile for a couple of days. So… Maybe in two days we can… Consummate." She smiled. "That sounds sort of royal. Doesn't it? Consummate." She laughed.

She was a strange woman. There were some exuberant, childlike things about her. And yet he sensed a deep pain. She had said she'd seen things.

But he wondered how…

He wondered if they were a bit more alike than perhaps it would seem on the surface.

"Tell me," he said. "Did you go to school?"

She shook her head. "No. Our education was easily seen to because everything we see we remember. By default, we learn a great many things quite quickly. But we were never around our peers. We never really had the chance to make friends with other people. We were… We were desperately cut off in many ways."

"Older and younger all at once," he said.

In some ways that echoed his own childhood. He had not had friends. He had worked.

He had learned to put his own needs, his own wants aside. There was no room for them. His father was woeful. His mother sad because her husband refused to do anything to lift them out of the dire straits they found themselves in. He had made her a servant, not a princess. He had done nothing that he had promised. And Acastus had to carry the weight of that.

Yes, he understood all too well.

"I suppose," she said. "When we got away we were like children. Eating candy, staying up as late as we wanted. Watching whatever we wanted on TV. We were free. And we took advantage of that."

"And then you took up gambling?"

"It was the best and easiest way for us to earn money using what talents we had. Like I said. We didn't go to school. We didn't have formal education. We didn't have anything when we escaped my father's compound. We didn't want to be outright con artists. But in a poker game, you feel as if people are consenting to being fleeced. At least, that's what we told ourselves. Jessie was the mastermind. For my part, I was the conscience. I didn't ever want us to go too far. Because I've always wondered, what is it that makes a man think he is above the laws of common decency? What is it that makes a man believe that he could hurt other people in pursuit of his own wealth?"

"I wonder that as well," he said. "For my part, I do not cause harm. I am far too familiar with powerful men who do."

He burned with no great conviction over that. But it was a decision that he had made.

Because he would differentiate himself from Stavros Argos. He differentiated himself from his father by taking action. But Stavros had enjoyed lording power over people, as much as he had enjoyed withholding it.

And that was never Acastus. And never would be.

He had always known this moment would come. This moment when he would marry a woman that he barely knew, and have an heir with her.

And yet now that he was here, it seemed a stranger thing than he had anticipated.

Perhaps because he was so attracted to her.

He had never been attracted in the same way to Elena Argos.

He had known her since she was a girl, but she had the same condescending manner that her father did, and while there had been a certain masculine drive to subdue that, mostly, he had found it repellent.

There was nothing about the Argos family that he liked, and the biggest issue with having a child with that family was that their blood would be mingled with his own.

In so many ways Stavros had handed him something better than he had before. While convincing himself that he was hurting Acastus. It was humorous.

Yes, he had won.

Maren Hargreave was beautiful. She wanted a

baby. And making that baby would be an entirely pleasant experience.

He would have to be slow with her. Gentle. He had not counted on her being untried, but he was happy to train her in the ways of pleasure between men and women.

He would not have to worry about her falling in love with him.

He was not fundamentally lovable.

"So you were robbing the rich and giving to the poor?" he asked.

"If you consider us the poor, yes. I would not call it overly altruistic, however. I'm not certain that we were… I think we were being good on a technicality. But it was important to me."

That didn't surprise him. It was that air of innocence that she had.

She was a beautiful thing.

And that sweetness appealed to him. Because he had exposure to so little of it. He didn't know how she managed to retain it. He certainly hadn't managed any.

"I'm glad," he said. "That you will be the mother of my child."

It seemed like a light had been switched on from inside of her. She positively glowed. "Really?"

"Yes," he said.

"Well, go on. You silly man. You can't say something like that and then not elaborate at great length. A person does like to be flattered."

"It is not flattery, but the truth. I think you will be able to teach the child what it means to be loved. That is something I would not be able to do."

"You don't think that you'd love a child?"

"I've seen no evidence that I am capable of finer feelings. I am driven, though. And I must hope that it is a fitting substitute."

"I do have one request," she said, looking down at her food. And then she looked back up at him. There was something about the way that she caught his eye. Beneath her lashes. Something bold and coy all at the same time. Innocence and sexuality radiating off of her in reckless waves.

"What is it, little one?" He didn't know why he added that tender phrase. He was not tender, and she should not become accustomed to the idea that he might be.

"I think I should like for you to seduce me."

She curled up in a ball on her bed, filled with a sense of cringe that she couldn't escape. Why had she said that to him?

She had kissed him. He had kissed her. But she had kissed him back. He had been... Glorious. Incredible. And she'd been so lost in that haze that then she had...

She'd asked him to seduce her.

*"Any special manner of seduction?"*

*"The seductive kind."*

And she shivered with the memory.

The seductive kind. She was an idiot. An outright absolute idiot. What was she thinking? Why was he like this?

She howled into her pillow.

It was interesting, that he hadn't been around children his own age either. But he didn't seem to suffer for it. Maren was very good at playing parts for short periods of time. She'd had to play the seductress on multiple occasions, but she never had to actually follow through with any of it. She never had to keep anything up for more than a couple of hours. If she put on makeup, and did her hair, or put a wig on, she could functionally make anything happen.

But now she had gone and begged her husband to seduce her. She told him that she didn't have any experience.

Why had she done that? Maybe she could have pretended to know what she was doing.

But why?

She sat up in bed. Yes. Why? This was an unexpected turn of events. Much like winning a castle. Much like becoming a princess. Why shouldn't it be about her? Why shouldn't it be about what she wanted? Her being a seductress might make him feel better, but what did she care about his feelings?

This wasn't about him. This was about her. He had his goals, and she had hers.

She wanted the sex to be a good memory. She wanted the experience to leave her enriched, rather than reduced. She wanted it to be a step forward into a different sort of life, a different sort of Maren. It made her excited to think about it. The opportunity to be a woman in these new faceted ways.

To explore her sexuality. To experience pregnancy, being a mother.

To be connected yet again to family.

And even though he wouldn't be her husband in truth, he was legally her husband, and they would be a family unit. He had promised protection. It was more than her own father had ever given. It mattered. It meant something. That was how she had to look at it. An opportunity. What was life if not a series of interesting opportunities? She had experienced a lot in her years. And she'd had the freedom to decide what she wanted to do for the last few years. If she'd wanted to, she could've gone out and gone clubbing every night. She could have sought anonymous pleasure with strangers. She had determined that wasn't for her.

She was much more interested in safety, security. Much more interested in the path she was on.

And so with confidence she could say she was going to claim it.

It was not very often that surprises in life came shaped like a six foot four muscular billionaire.

It was a pleasant one, as they went.

As long as she didn't expect anything from him but... Pleasure. And money apparently. She wasn't too broken up about the money.

She wondered *how* he might seduce her. And when he might start.

She fell asleep on tenterhooks, waiting for that, but he didn't come to her room.

But then, that was for the best. She had the idea that she wanted the seduction to be something more. Something a bit gentle. Something to ease her in.

She dressed in a flowing gown and went downstairs, heading toward the parlor where her large sitting cushions were. She only wanted pastries and some coffee, she did not need the whole dining table for that. But she was surprised to find coffee and pastries waiting for her in that very room when she arrived.

And then even more surprised to see him sitting there, reading a book.

"Good morning," he said.

"Good morning, Acastus," she said. "I'm surprised to see you here."

"Are you? I anticipated that you would wish to break your fast here. And that you would probably want something sweet."

She narrowed her eyes. "I see. And how do you know that?"

"I spent a collective two hours speaking to you yesterday, and you think that you might remain unknowable to me? You asked for a seduction, Maren Hargreave. Did you think that I would be anything less than thorough in it?"

"As seduction goes," she said, taking her seat on one of the large cushions and reaching for a flaky, glazed pastry, "you're not far off that the way to my heart is paved with butter."

"But it wasn't to reach your heart, darling. Just that tender place between your thighs."

And she felt an answering pulse quicken down there. Just where he'd said. It should be crass and vulgar. But there was something about how he said it, while sitting there with his large masculine hands caressing the spine of that poor book, that made her feel… Not offended. Not disgusted. In fact, she felt as if she could feel the way his fingertips might trail down her own spine. And shamefully, wondered how they would feel where she was growing a bit wet for him.

"Well. But it probably works there too."

She took a bite of the pastry. It was incredible.

"It's very sweet the way that you blush."

"I told you," she said, yet again opting for honesty. "I haven't any experience with men. All I know about sex I have learned from books and movies.

Don't get me wrong. I have vivid images stored in my mind. And so it will be up to you to reach deep for my fantasies I suppose."

"Too easy," he said.

"Is it?"

"Yes. You are sweet. In spite of all the things that have happened to you. But you're also very strong, and a lesser man might miss that. He might think that you are soft, and therefore easily crushed. I do not think so. You are soft, it is true, but that is a choice. And it's one you've made from a position of strength. You need a man who can match your strength. You would never respect a man who didn't. You also see the difference between a bully and a man who is strong. Truly strong. You do not wish for someone to overpower you. You wish for strength to surrender to. And those are very different things."

Her heart fluttered. "I have never surrendered in my life."

"No, of course not. Because in the past when men or anyone else has demanded surrender of you, they did so because they wished to see you reduced. You want to give surrender joyfully. You wish to place that surrender in the hands of someone who will treat it well. Who wishes to take it and use your vulnerability as a way to access your pleasure. That's what you have protected all this time. Because you know that when you do surrender, it will be total. Complete. You will not lie back and part your legs for a man who would use his strength to dishonor that which you are offering. And I will not. I will see it as the gift that it is. That each and every cry of delight is being given to me freely. A gift that I could never hope to earn, but must take it as something freely presented and given. Any power I have over you, over your body, is because you have given it to me. Even now. Yes, I married you by default. There is power in that. But I could never take you if you did not give yourself. Because that is not the kind of man I am. That is not what power means to me. To physically force is the domain of the weak. True strength is in waiting. True strength is in knowing that the only way to truly win is to have earned a forfeit."

"All very sexy," she said, her throat feeling parched. "And admirable in part. But why is sex a forfeit for a woman and a victory for a man?"

He leaned forward. "It is an exchange. When I strip you of your clothes, when I lower my head to take one of your begging nipples into my mouth, when I kiss my way down your stomach and taste that sweet honey between your legs, I will be revealing myself. My fantasies will show you the deepest part of myself. As I take control I surrender my power. If you do not capitulate, if you do not find pleasure, then I am a failure. The captain of the ship steers it through the storm, does he not? He is the master, and yet. If the sea overtakes him, if he fails, he goes down with the ship. In that sense, the power goes to you. All of it. By claiming authority, by claiming dominion, in effect, I give you the power to destroy me. You may find me wanting. You may refuse me. And then it is I who have opened up the deep and secret places inside of himself to find them rejected."

His words rolled over her, and she found she had to think on them. Deeply.

And yet they made sense. The greater power a person assumed, the more they had to lose.

By offering her the position of submission, he was in effect granting her the power to wholesale demolish the dominance he tried to claim. And that was to risk humiliation. One thing she did know, was that there was little more devastating for a man. And so she could see that the risk was high.

She was discomfited, by how well he read her. By just how deeply he seemed to understand her concern about the risk of all this. By how deeply he seemed to understand her. When they had only just barely met.

She looked at him, the hard cut of his face. The lean, stock lines of his body.

This morning, he was casual. His white shirt unbuttoned at the throat, his sleeves rolled up past his elbows.

His forearms were delicious, well-defined and muscular.

He was truly a sight to behold. His emotions were complicated. But she looked into his eyes, and tried to pull them apart anyway. Yes, there was a coldness to him, but there was a heat as well. No one could lay claim to this level of sensual knowledge without heat.

"If I were to leave out breakfast for you it would be strong espresso. You do not wish to have sweets in the morning. You would rather have… Nothing, actually, if you took your pick. But if there was a breakfast to be put before you, it would be eggs. Bacon, likely. American bacon. You would not freely admit that. You do not like relationships because you did not learn how to have them. But you do enjoy sex because it allows you to connect with someone. If you put yourself in the dominant position to a woman's needs then you must stop and read her. And that allows you a feeling of intimacy without having actually achieved it. A surrogate for what other humans are looking for in life. But you're comfortable with the surrogacy." She could see disquiet in his dark eyes. "Oh, it isn't that you've never made a connection. You have one. And it is so domineering, so all-consuming, that you cannot afford another."

One of the ways that she and Jessie had tried to make money at first was by claiming that Maren was a psychic. But she had become uncomfortable with that quickly. She was not a psychic. She was simply astute at reading people. And one thing she had never wanted to do was take advantage of someone's pain. And when you got into faux psychic readings you were invariably brushing up against extremely personal things.

But she used those tricks now, to delve into him. Every remark created a microexpression on his face. A reaction that most anyone else would never notice. But that she did.

"You don't have to tell me that I'm correct," she said. "I can see that I am."

"That is quite the parlor trick," he said.

"I know," she said. "It's all just paying attention. I appreciate that you did not bother to deny it."

"And why bother to deny it?" He shrugged. "You are my wife. By default, the closest, most binding relationship I have save family."

"And your remaining family is your mother. Your father was an ineffective fool," she said, paraphrasing his own words back to him. "You had to take care of her. And you still do. You're a good son. Because you love your mother, and also because you're angry at your father. And the better you are at being a son, the more insipid he looks by his inability to do what a man ought to have done. You are twice the man he was. If not more. Before the breakfast that you prefer not to eat every day."

"Well spotted," he said. "That is all true. Except the part about wishing to have intimate connections and not having the energy for them. I don't want them. I don't want them, because love is a cage. My mother was kept in that cage for twenty-five years.

Miserable. I do know, the older I get the more I realize my father was trapped in it as well. He loved my mother. He was just far too ineffective to do it well. What is worse than that? To love a woman, and to track her into your poorly constructed facsimile of how you express that love. I would never. And so I prefer honesty. And sex. Bodies are honest."

Her own felt strung out. Sparring with men had always been something she'd enjoyed. It always felt a bit dangerous, a bit like foreplay, if she were honest. Most of the time, her marks were men she did not find attractive, but on the rare occasions when she had, she had found the process invigorating. She had told herself on more than one occasion that her verbal sparring could be a substitute for sex. She had often found herself aroused by it. And so to bring it into this discussion, with the man she had married, a man whose bed she was going to share, put her on edge in a way she never had been before.

It affected her physically.

It filled her with desire.

"And what else is planned for my seduction today?" she asked.

"You are a woman who likes to know things. Everything. I wonder what it would be like for you if a silken blindfold covered your eyes and you had to simply feel."

The image, of being blindfolded while she waited

to find out where he might touch her next, kissed her next, flooded her.

And she felt an answering wetness between her legs.

"I have no interest in any such thing."

"You're a liar. And I don't know what you get out of being a liar on this score. Perhaps you are embarrassed. To tell me your true, sensual nature. You repressed it long enough."

"I'm not embarrassed," she protested. Even while a pulse throbbed between her thighs that shamed her, and called her a liar.

Maybe this was the problem. She was ashamed because she wanted to sleep with him. Because she didn't even think she wanted to wait until tomorrow when she was actually fertile to be with him.

Because she was curious. Because she was attracted to him, in spite of the fact that she didn't love him.

Was this her own fear of wickedness?

Her own hang-ups? Why would she think that?

Of course she had grown up taking on board a somewhat misogynistic attitude around women. Her father had not respected them. He had seen women only as pawns. As sexual objects. And she could see the way that he had treated women he thought of as smart, and women he thought of as playthings. She and Jessie had played into those sorts of perceptions. They had made themselves into the kind of women

who looked like they could be treated as sexual objects, but who were in fact smart, as if those two
things were entirely separate, when she knew they
weren't. They were playing games. They were using
people's prejudices against them, and yet, she was
struck just then by how much it had sunk into her
own bones. How much of it lived inside of her.

That she felt she had to be a fake sort of sexy, con-
cealing her brilliance. Instead of acknowledging that
she liked to be beautiful. That she wanted to be sexy.
And that it didn't make her less smart.

That she could be all those things. And still good.

There had been such a great many traumatic
things for her to work out upon leaving her father's
compound, that she had missed this one.

She wondered how many more she'd missed.

"All right. Perhaps I would like to be blindfolded."
A luxurious image filled her mind, one that made
her blush. "You could surprise me."

Her deep and real fantasy was him pressing the
most intimate part of himself to her mouth, and her
taking him in deep.

It made her feel overheated.

And she fought against shame.

"You have sex with strangers often, don't you?"

"When it suits me," he said. "I don't know what
you would define as *often*."

"You feel no shame about it," she said.

"No. I feel no shame around the way I conduct

myself in life, and I have worked hard to arrive at such a place. I am not my father. I take ownership of that which I am. I make no promises I cannot keep. And I act with a clean conscience. When I have sex, it is with a woman who wants what I want. I am clear and I am up front. And so I feel no need for shame."

"I'm fighting shame," she said. "Because your kiss awoke desire within me, and it makes me feel as if I am not good. Because wicked women crave the bodies of men they don't know. That they don't love. I made that rule, for myself and for Jessie, to protect us. Because I didn't want to make love to a man, fall in love with him, and have him leave only to be haunted by the images of us in bed together. But perhaps that was a lie. Perhaps I simply felt dirty. From my time spent conning people. From the time I spent growing up in my father's house. And I was afraid of adding another sin to my roster. But I do not wish to see this as a sin. I want you."

"That must be a record. The seduction has only lasted these past twenty minutes."

"I should like you to keep on seducing me. I want to be mindless with it." She smiled. "I'm never mindless, you see. I am both fascinated by and afraid at the idea that a man might be able to make me so."

"Then the seduction will continue, wife. Until you cannot resist."

# CHAPTER FIVE

THERE WAS A full staff at the palace to see to Maren's every whim and desire. But Acastus decided that he would fulfill them himself. He had decided that he would become the fulfillment of all that she desired, because he wished that surrender. More than he would've said that morning. What he had intended as a game had turned into something much more real. Much more honest.

He went over the dossier that she had sent to the palace staff. The one that stated all of her preferences. Her favorite foods, her favorite music.

And he packed them a picnic lunch, in accordance with her wishes. He did all of the preparation for the food himself.

He programmed a playlist to his phone, and packed a small speaker into the bag because that would add to it. To the sense of knowing her. And he could see that it was important to her. She was a discomfiting creature. The way that she had succinctly analyzed him had cut. But it was no secret. He was proud of the way that he had cared for his mother. She read him wrong if she thought that he feared anything, but he could see how with many other people that would be true. He personally just did not find use for emotion.

There was no room in his life for it, and so he did not give it space. That was practical. It was not a weakness.

He prized strength above all else.

And as long as he had strength enough to fulfill his obligations, there could be no sense of failure in him.

By the time he found Maren again, she was back in the sitting room, curled up on a cushion, reading a book.

He could see that it was a romance. The problem with her was that she did seem quite soft. He did not wish to hurt her, in the way that he simply could not respect men who harmed women. Stavros Argos was the sort of man who hurt women with malicious cruelty. He'd enjoyed the despair of Acastus's mother. He'd seen his own daughter as a pawn to be manipulated and his wife as little more than an accessory. His father was the sort of man who hurt a woman with apathy. And both of those things were quite powerful and quite real. He despised it.

But he had laid out his reality to Maren quite

firmly. He could only hope that she listened. That she understood.

It was important that she did.

"I have packed us a picnic lunch," he said.

"You did? Or did you have Iliana ask one of the kitchen workers to—"

"I did," he said. "I think you will find that many of your favorites are in there. Come. Let us go outside. There is a lovely spot overlooking the sea."

"Every spot overlooks the sea," she said, the bit of edge in her voice the only thing that betrayed her wariness.

"Yes. It does. This is part of your seduction, do not look at me as if I am trying to trick you."

"I'm sorry. Everything in my life at one time was a con. I suppose I'm always waiting for the other shoe to drop."

"And who could blame you. But I am simply doing as you asked. And if it is working, then I am only giving to you. Surrendering to you in that sense. The exchange. You will recall."

That earned him a slight smile.

She had changed into a rather diaphanous white dress, and it conformed to her curves. When she stood, he felt as if he had been punched low in the stomach.

He really had not counted on her beauty. It was arresting. Magnificent. As was she.

He was seducing her, but one thing was certain, she was doing a fair enough job of seducing him.

He was anticipating the time they would come together more than he had anticipated. He had truly believed that this would all be about conceiving the child for him. But suddenly it had been reduced to this. To her.

They walked out of the palace, and were greeted by the intensity of the turquoise sea.

He had grown up here. He knew exactly where to take her.

There was a small patch of grass up on top of one of the craggy rocks, and it overlooked the ocean. One of the only good places to sit outside. He helped her up the side of the craggy stones, and placed the picnic basket between them when they sat on the pad of grass.

"This is lovely," she said, and then she opened up the picnic basket. "What is this?" She took out the speaker.

"As much as I enjoy the sounds of the sea, I did think that perhaps you would like an aria."

He began to play the music. Her favorite opera. Which he had found she was a fan of, through the dossier.

"You read my file," she said. She dug through the basket deeper. And took out a toaster pastry. "You really did read my file." But she looked delighted.

"I did. I wished to give you an afternoon specifically suited to your desires."

She shook her head and laughed. "And what about yours?"

"I am looking at you lit in the golden light from the sun. What could I desire more? Except that you strip your dress off, so that I could see the glory of your bare body beneath the sunlight. But that perhaps will be for another time."

She turned pink. And he could see that she was annoyed by it.

"You are not subtle at all."

"You don't want subtlety," he said. "You wish to be adored."

He meant to say it somewhat as a joke. But as soon as he said the words, he could see how true they were. Had anyone ever worshipped her? There had been no lover, so she had not been worshipped in that way. Her father had been a cruel man. Her mother had left. She had a sister, but that was not the same sort of relationship. No. No one had ever worshipped her. Adored her. And he could see she was desperately hungry for it.

"Well, thank you," she said. "This is very thoughtful. I've never been on a date before."

She leaned over and bumped her shoulder against his, smiling up at him. It was... Extraordinarily cute and he had no idea what to do with it.

"I don't know this is a date," he said.

She reached into the basket again and took out a grilled cheese sandwich. She was delighted to find it. She took a happy bite of it.

"It is a date. We are on a date. Which is good. Because even though sleeping with you after one date will be slightly promiscuous of me, at least you have taken me out."

"To a patch of grass."

"Indeed."

"I didn't think you were worrying about whether or not you were promiscuous. Besides, I am your husband."

That created a glowing light in her eyes that he had to turn away from.

"Yes," she said softly. "You are."

She was his wife. His wife. And that should mean very little. It was a formality. It was her instead of Elena Argos, a substitute. It mattered not.

And yet he found that he was glad he was here with Maren and not Elena.

What a strange, strange thing.

And perhaps it was merely sexual desire.

Because sexual desire was a powerful thing, and he was only a man.

Maybe it was as simple as that.

"So what's your sign?" She looked up at him, and batted her eyes.

"Are you kidding?"

"Yes," she said. "I googled you. I already know your birthday. You're a Taurus. Obviously."

"What does that mean?"

"It doesn't really matter, it's just fun to watch you react to it."

"You are a brat," he said.

She laughed. "My sister has called me that before. But nobody else. I guess no one else knows me well enough."

And she wanted someone to know her, he could see that too.

This was all in aid of seduction. He would do well to remember that. He didn't need to grow an attachment to this strange creature that he had married.

He took his own sandwich, and ate it while he watched her.

She really was a sight to behold, bright and red and gold against this extraordinary scenery behind her. All that blue.

"Did you live near the sea growing up?"

She shook her head. "This is glorious. I'm from the US, obviously. But we did spend part of our childhood in London, and then most of our years since have been in England. We've traveled. But places like Las Vegas. I have always liked the idea of living somewhere where there was sun. Where it was a bit brighter. A bit warmer. I like this ocean, even if I do sometimes enjoy the stormy gray sea. All of it's beautiful. But mostly, just having something of my own is beautiful. Though I guess we share it." She frowned. "Life is strange. It's never quite as straightforward as you hope it might be."

"Life is filled with hooks. You just have to decide what to do with the particular ones you get caught on."

"I suppose that is true. There is no such thing as true freedom. The only thing that comes close is being a sociopath like my father was. You are free of obligation. Both to society and to anyone who might care for you. Anyone you should care for. But then there is the law. And it always catches up to you. In the end."

"Do you believe that?" he asked.

"I've seen it. My father is dead because of it."

He could not figure out what the appropriate response was to that. "I'm sorry."

She frowned. "In many ways I'm not. And yet in some ways… You know it's very unsatisfying when a villain meets his end. Especially when they never cared if they were the villain. Not even a little. Especially when they were only ever interested in themselves. In their own victories. I find it very unsatisfying to think that he might just be gone. But that was the end for him. And he never once knew what a terrible person he was. I need to believe that there's recompense in the afterlife."

"I suppose I do too," he said. He had never even had that thought fully formed inside of him, much less spoken aloud to another person. "The idea that my father lived and died a weak man, and never truly understood the harm that he caused... And never got to witness the way that I fixed it... It is a deeply unsatisfying one. I reject it. I need to believe he suffers."

"Me too. Maybe they're together. Maybe they're watching us eat very good grilled cheese while the flames of hell touch their feet."

"Probably the strangest date conversation anyone has ever had," he said.

"Probably," she agreed. "But I do not suppose you or I were ever destined for normal."

"No indeed."

"I would like normal. Birthday parties and friends and Christmas."

"Christmas?"

"I never really had it. And I'd like to decorate the palace, from top to bottom. I ordered decorations before I arrived and had them stored for the season. I've always wanted...that sparkle. That magic."

She put her sandwich down, and then surprised him by putting her hand on his face. He didn't move. He simply allowed her to lean in and press a kiss to his lips. It was slow, methodical. Lovely. His whole body burned with it. With her.

He had set out to seduce her. But she was doing something to him. It was the artlessness. And the insight. Such a strange combination of things for a person to possess. Her kiss was cool, inexperienced. Tender. And it ignited him in a way that nothing else ever had.

He took a lock of her hair and wrapped it around his finger. Tested the silken nest of her hair between his fingertips.

"Let me bathe you," he said.

"What?"

"I will not claim you until tomorrow, but tonight… Let me wash your hair. Let me touch your skin, slick with water."

He did not know why he was making this request. He felt undone. And he had never felt undone in his life.

"Yes," she whispered.

He had won a victory. Or perhaps he had not.

The exchange of power between the two of them was so profound, that he realized he might as well be on his knees.

Normally he would turn away from it.

But not here. Not with her. Because it was simply not like anything he had ever experienced. Because there were rules. Firmly set rules. And so at least this would end. Perhaps it was a chance for both of them to indulge, when they otherwise would not.

Tonight…

His body was tight with anticipation. He could not remember the last time he had truly seduced a woman. He wondered if he ever had.

Women had wanted him, that was certain. But this was different. This was about finding her specific desires, her specific needs, and bending them to his will.

Tonight.

And the very thought of it made him feel like fire.

# CHAPTER SIX

SHE DIDN'T KNOW what to expect. She had been sitting in her room wearing only a robe for the past hour, pacing. He had not joined her for dinner, and she felt that it was on purpose. He had not joined her for dinner, and she felt that it was because he was trying to heighten her anticipation.

She had not expected the show of…humanity today. The way he had given her her favorite foods. The way he had played her favorite music. Talked to her. Listened to her. And then ended it with a promise to…

To bathe her.

Her heart was fluttering.

He had said that they wouldn't consummate tonight.

She was still a jangle of nerves.

She knew that men liked the look of her body when it was clothed. She imagined that he would like it naked.

But the fact remained this was new territory for her, and it was a bit…

Well, it was more than a little bit enervating.

She hadn't expected this as a seduction. She wasn't sure what she had expected a seduction to be. She only knew that this felt especially… Luxurious. Sensual. Arousing.

He had found it. The way to get to her. He had lavished her with attention earlier, and then withheld it. She was poised on the edge of a knife. She didn't know how to imagine what was going to come next. She had no picture in her head.

That bastard had read her like a book. And instantly she was brought back to the way that he had caressed the spine of the book this morning.

*Oh, my.*

There was a soft knock at the door and she jumped. It was him, she knew. She hadn't expected him to knock. She had a feeling he knew that, and it was why he had done so. He was trying to get around her expectations. Trying to defy what she might think of him.

She opened up the door. And her heart did a complicated dance in her rib cage.

He still had on that white shirt, but another button was undone. The sleeves were rolled up. His feet were bare.

The lateness of the day saw his jaw more shadowed, rough looking. She wished to touch it again. To touch him.

But she decided to surrender to his power. To give in to him completely. To allow him to direct this. To place her pleasure in his hands, because he had promised it would make her powerful, and so she would trust it. Would give it.

"I wondered when you would come," she said.

His lips curved. "And I wonder when you will."

She blinked. "What? *Oh*." It took her a second.

Her stomach went tight.

"Come, little one, I have drawn a bath for you already."

He led her through her vast wardrobe room, and into the bathroom. Which was a stunning, luxurious space. The bath itself was like a large ornate bowl, with golden feet, and a cushioned place for her to rest her head.

She looked at him, holding the edges of her robe together.

"No modesty with me, darling. Show me all that you are. It will be my undoing."

Power.

To claim power, she had to be vulnerable.

It made sense then. Clicked into place. And she found herself moving her hands to the knot on her belt. Undoing it. And then letting her robe slide off of her body and pool down on the floor.

In an instant, she saw each of his reactions, the

way that he sucked in a hard breath, the slight clench of his fist. She could see his midsection go tight beneath his shirt, could see his pulse pound harder at his throat. His teeth were locked together, the fire burning bright in his eyes.

It was as if his entire body had gotten just a bit harder. As if he was holding on to his composure with that much more of a struggle.

They had traded. She had given. And it had taken something from him.

She was exhilarated by it.

"Goddess," he said. "Venus. My culture has for thousands of years had a great love of sensuality. Of beauty. You would be the sort of beauty that they wrote epics about."

"How fortunate for me, though I do not wish to be the start of a war, even a mythical one."

"And yet I imagine you could've started many. If you chose."

"I try to use my powers for good. Mostly. I haven't always."

"Did you make men think that they could earn the night in your bed, but con them into trading their money to you instead?"

"Not as such," she said, almost forgetting for a moment that she was standing there naked until she became unbearably conscious of the ache in her breasts, the way that her nipples went tight. "But I did… I suppose I've used my beauty to distract men before. Is it my fault, though, that they underestimate a woman? Especially if she has…" She cupped her own breasts and took a chance, rubbing her thumb over one of her nipples. He clenched his fists all the way.

"Shall I help you into the bath?"

"Please."

He took a step closer to her, and then he pressed his fingertip between her shoulder blades, drawing it all the way down the line of her spine. The images from this morning were overlaid on the moment, her breasts catching in her chest, her whole body poised on the edge of a knife.

He did not have to speak the words, she could feel them. He had read her like that book. He knew her. What she wanted. What she craved. She was used to knowing other people in this way, but she did not know what it was to be known by someone else. She could not decide if it was terrifying or exhilarating.

She decided it was both.

He picked her up, and the heat of his body burned her through his clothes. His bare hands, one resting on her rib cage near the swell of her breasts, and the other around her thigh, set her pulse on fire.

And then he set her down gently into the warm water, and knelt by the tub.

"Glorious," he whispered. He moved his hands down into the water and took a handful of it, pouring it out over her breasts.

"Oh," she said, the shock of pleasure moving through her.

"Tomorrow, my mouth will be there."

"Yes," she whispered.

But why tomorrow? Why not *now*?

She wanted him.

For once in her life, she wasn't worried about the future. What she would remember. What might haunt her. For once she was only worried about what she wanted. And it was right there. Within reach. But then she did not have a chance to ponder it because he picked up a bar of soap and slicked his hands with it before moving them down over her breasts, down her midsection and back up again, paying special attention to her nipples as he skimmed his thumbs over her sensitized flesh.

"Acastus," she gasped.

"Yes," he ground out. "So responsive. So lovely. You are absolutely perfect. Gorgeous, my girl."

She had never been anyone's girl. Not in so long. And never like this.

She felt small and fragile and protected.

Safe.

And it made her want to weep. How could this dangerous predator of a man make her feel safe?

How could his touch be so gentle when his hands were so strong?

He continued to smooth his palms over her body,

and then his hands found that place between her thighs and began to stroke her.

She gripped the edge of the bathtub, arching her hips in time with his touch.

"You were wet for me," he said.

"Yes," she whispered.

"So wet."

"Yes," she agreed.

"Because you are a good girl. And you will get what you want. You will get what you need."

She wanted to weep. The affirmations did something to her, reached inside of her and tangled around all of these needy places that she had never known existed. Or at least that she tried to hide. Even from herself.

Because she had been worried, hadn't she? That she wasn't good. That something was wrong with her.

He was making this feel okay. He was making it feel right. He was making it feel good.

Making her feel good.

She began to whimper.

And then he cursed, moving his hand from between her legs.

"I was going to wait," he growled.

But then he claimed her mouth with his, and she found herself being lifted from the water.

Her naked body pressed against his clothed one, leaving water bleeding into the fabric.

"I must have you," he said. "I must."

She couldn't protest.

He lifted her up onto the counter, and stepped between her open thighs, and she could feel the hardness of him pressing there to the heart of her.

She kissed him, pushing her fingers through his hair.

Then he lowered his head and sucked her nipple into his mouth as he had promised to do tomorrow.

She didn't want to wait.

His tongue played havoc with her, and then he moved his attentions down her midsection, dropped to his knees before her and cupped her backside in his large hands, pulling her toward his mouth.

And he consumed her. He looked up at her, his dark eyes meeting hers. "I gave you your favorite treats earlier. And now I shall have mine." Then he licked her. Deep. Hard. As if he was tasting the most gloriously sweet dessert he'd ever had in his life.

He devoured her.

And she was overcome.

She arched her hips into his seeking tongue, and surrendered herself.

She was lost in the sensations. Lost in him. Whimpering in the back of her throat as he sucked that sensitive bundle of nerves between his lips, as his hand joined his mouth, as he pushed a finger deep within her while he continued to play havoc on her body.

And then she shattered. Utterly and completely.

The orgasm that crashed over her unlike anything she'd experienced by her own hand. It surpassed the descriptions of things that she'd read about. It was a breaking apart. A storm-tossed sea. It was fireworks and waves. It was everything she had ever read and somehow more. Coming from deep within her and overtaking her completely. Making her mind, that cluttered, eternally seeking place, into a desolate wasteland. Into nothing more than her need.

Into nothing more than the pleasure that was washing over her.

She was remade.

In that moment.

Not a brain containing endless images. But a body. Seeking, releasing, having.

And then he moved back up and kissed her mouth, holding her fast to him while he pushed his fingers through her hair and held her head steady, kissing deeper and deeper as the last vestiges of her orgasm shuddered through her.

"Acastus," she whispered. "My husband."

"You are so beautiful," he said. "So beautiful." He smoothed his thumb over her lips, and she had never felt so desired. So wanted. So wholly approved of in all of her life. And she did not worry about what it might mean. She simply reveled in it. Accepted it. Became overjoyed with it.

It was like she was bathed in a glow. One that suffused her entire being.

"I did not intend for it to go this far. Forgive me."

"You don't need…"

But then suddenly he was moving away from her. Leaving her.

"Tomorrow," he said. "As planned."

And she could sense that… He was ashamed. That he had deviated from the plan. That he needed to do this, to regroup, to regain some of his control.

And it made her feel bereft. Because she was lost. Out of her mind. And she wanted for him to be as well.

And when he left, she felt like he had taken a piece of her with him.

And all the warmth she felt moments before went out.

## CHAPTER SEVEN

HE HAD GONE too far. He had meant to maintain his control. He had meant to make it about her. He had not meant to push her so far. He had not meant…

He was overwrought. And he was never over-wrought. He never had feelings that he could not gain dominion over. And here he was. Shaking over a virgin.

He was…

He had to leave her. He had to defer his own plea-sure. Because otherwise…

He would fail the test of control. And he could not have that.

He went to the bar in his room and poured him-self a measure of whiskey.

And he nearly laughed when he lifted the glass to his lips and the liquor touched his tongue, only to have the door open.

And there she was. Wearing a lace gown he could see through. And even if he could not, he would al-ways see her as naked in his mind.

Pale, glorious breasts tipped with strawberry-colored nipples. That thatch of red hair between her legs. Yes, he would always see that.

But she was showing him anyway.

"I do not wish to stop," she said. "And I have decided that this is a gift, this marriage. That I get to have something that I thought that I would be denied all of my life. I desire you. I want you inside me."

He had lost. He knew that. If this was a war, then this battle went to her.

He would not deny her. He could not.

It was symbolic, anyway. His show of resistance.

But in his dominance he had shown his weakness.

He had taken her and held her and pleasured her, and it only showed his own lack of resistance. She saw that. And she was using it against him. He could not blame her.

He wanted her. Craved her.

And here she was before him, her curves barely contained, asking that he be inside of her.

His body throbbed in response.

This was insanity, but it would be days of it. And then he would go back to his life and wait to find out if she was carrying his child or not. If so he would come back for a few more days of it.

That was all. There were limits to it. There were limits.

*And here you are moving the boundaries. Because of your own weakness.*

He snarled, and set the whiskey down. He closed the space between them and wrapped his arm around her waist, drawing her up against his body. "You want me like this? On edge? Barely in control of myself? Is that what you want?"

"Yes. It is what I want, my husband. I'm surrendering to you. To this. Your seduction was thorough."

"As was yours," he said, moving his hand down to cup her backside. He squeezed her hard. "I am a man who prizes control above all else. I indulge, but only when I mean to. You have pushed me. I did not need to do this. I did not intend to be with you like this tonight. But I cannot resist you. How does that make you feel?"

"Powerful," she whispered. "And weak at once. What if I don't please you?"

"You cannot help but please me. Please me by your very form. You please me in all ways."

The words tumbled from his lips, as close to poetry as he had ever gotten. "My princess."

She was a princess, and he the Prince. And yet that did not feel like the achievement here. The achievement was holding her in his arms.

It was as if the world had shrunk, to this palace on the rock, but maybe even more so, to this room. To them.

And nothing more.

He grabbed the straps of the lace dress and pulled them down, revealing her breasts to his hungry gaze, and then he revealed the rest of her body. She was naked again before him, but her own eyes were seeking.

"I wish to see you," she said. "All of you."

And there was something particularly laser focused to her gaze, something that reached down deep into his gut and twisted hard. She would not forget a single detail of his body.

He was not a shy man, he was comfortable with himself.

But what a strange moment, knowing he would reveal himself to a woman who would forever remember him like this. Remember this encounter. Every detail of it burned into her brain. It had to be good. Everything. All that he gave her.

He was not a man given to performance anxiety. He would rise to the challenge.

Because she deserved it.

She had not asked for this. And yet she was here. His equal in this moment in a profound way. Seeing all that this alliance offered her and taking it. But more than that, seizing the sensual opportunity that existed between them. It was a glorious thing.

He moved his hands to the buttons on his shirt and undid them, casting it to the floor, and he watched with satisfaction as desire illuminated her eyes.

"Have you seen a naked man?"

"Not in person," she said. "You will be my first. My standard."

She said first in that there would be more, and right then he felt that was unacceptable. But of course, the parameters he laid down for their marriage would suggest that they would take other lovers.

Later. He would deal with that later. He would focus now on being so undeniable that she would never want anyone else.

He moved his pants then, took them off along with his underwear, and watched as her eyes slid over every detail. He could feel her as if she had cupped his length and run her finger along it, so keen was her examination of him.

"You are quite a bit bigger than I expected," she said. "But I find that excites me."

He gritted his teeth against the onslaught of desire that created inside of him. He should find it embarrassing to respond to such a basic provocation. And yet, he found that with her, he was nothing more than an extremely basic man. He was nothing more than his own need. Nothing more than a cascade of desire coursing through him like a storm.

He needed her.

And then, she moved to kiss him, pressing her breasts to his chest, the length of her naked body up against his own creating a maelstrom of need inside of him. He held her fast. Clutching her hips and grinding his hardness against her softness.

She kissed his neck, peppered kisses down his

chest, and his heart reacted. His whole body reacted. She moved down, trailing her tongue along his abdominal muscles, and pausing at the head of his shaft. She pressed her lips against it, near featherlight, and all the more impacting for it.

And then she parted her lips and took him inside.

Her movements were unpracticed, unskilled, but glorious.

He arched his hips forward, and pushed himself a bit deeper, and she responded with enthusiasm. Working her hand in time with her mouth, doing her best to take as much of him as she could.

It was an out-of-body experience, a moment he would never be able to explain. It was for her, she had said. And yet it felt as if it was for him. And he had done nothing to deserve this. This was not in aid of making a child. This was simply them. Need and glory cascading between them. Both of them unable to deny it.

He felt a gathering desire at the base of his spine. Felt as if he would not be able to deny her any longer.

As if he would not be able to deny himself.

"Enough," he said gruffly, moving her away from him and picking her up, carrying her over to the bed.

He laid her down on it, and stood back, looking at the way her red hair flowed over the fine, black silk blankets.

She was so pale against the darkness. So beautiful.

He gripped his own shaft hard and squeezed it.

Trying to regain control of himself. Her eyes were hungry on him, and he did not see nerves. He saw only lust. Only need. Only desire gripping her, the same that it gripped him.

He moved to the bed, kissed her mouth and put his hand between her legs, stroking her until he had her in another sensual frenzy. Until she was wet. Until he could easily push two fingers deep inside of her.

He did not wish to cause her pain.

And perhaps a certain degree was inevitable. But he wanted this to be good. For her. He worked his fingers in and out of her body until she was shivering. Shaking.

Until a slow, deep orgasm rolled over her that squeezed him tight.

His name was on her lips as he positioned himself between her thighs and pressed the head of his arousal against her. Then he sank slowly inside of her. Inch by agonizing inch, the control that it took to not burst there and then was something he would've thought beyond him.

And when he was fully within her, he felt something like completion that he had never known before.

Something like home.

He had been a boy on his hands and knees in this place. A boy who scrubbed floors, who had spent time in the dungeon. And now he was in a bedroom, in a big, glorious bed, deep inside the castle's

Princess. And he could not make that matter. Because what mattered was her. What mattered was this. And them.

He arched forward, then withdrew, thrusting back inside of her, in a hard, firm stroke. She gasped, but arched her breasts up against him, indicating pleasure.

And then he was lost. In this. In her. He thrust in and out of her glorious body, watching the shifts and changes of her face, listening as her kitten-like sounds of desire began to intensify.

She clung to his shoulders, dug her fingernails into his skin, pain became pleasure. And they became one.

They moved together. In tandem with the storm.

And when his own climax burst over him, hers broke as well. He poured himself within her, as she squeezed him tight, crying out his name.

And when it was done, he felt as if something in him had changed.

But he was made of stone. So that could not be.

She did not leave his bed. Not for the next two days. Food was brought, left outside the door, and she couldn't even be embarrassed by all of it.

She felt like she should be. Maybe. Like she should be ashamed that she had surrendered herself to this thing between them with quite so much enthusiasm, but she could not find the shame.

She could find nothing but joy as he claimed her, over and over again. As he showed her new things that her body could do. New things that she could want. He had shown her a depth of need and sexual liberty inside of her own self that she just hadn't known could ever be there.

They had done things she didn't think she would ever want to do. More than that, she had begged for them.

Her cheeks heated at the memory. They had done things that weren't in aid of making a baby. Just for indulgence's sake. And it had been glorious.

It was why on the third day, when she woke up and found him getting dressed, she felt like she had been struck.

"What are you doing?" she asked sleepily from the bed.

"I'm on my way back to Athens," he said. "You will keep me informed as to whether or not you've conceived."

And there he was, the stranger. The man she had first seen lying in this very bed, when she had first arrived. Not the man who'd become her lover these last days. Not the man that she had convinced herself she had a connection with.

She had lost herself. She was a fool and she wanted to weep with it. Because what had she been thinking?

She had let herself get sucked into all this. She

should hope that she was pregnant. She did hope that she was pregnant. That they wouldn't have to do this again.

Because as he packed up and left, no affection, no kiss goodbye, she felt defeated. Small.

She wouldn't be able to endure this again.

Maren remembered being left. Her mother had done it. In some ways, even though it wasn't fair, even though Maren was the one who'd moved to the middle of the sea, she'd felt like Jessie had left her when she'd fallen in love with Ewan.

That spot inside her was sore, and him leaving pressed into it, like someone pushing their thumb against soft, overripe fruit.

She was alone. Again.

After that closeness, that bliss, it seemed especially cruel.

He didn't make any contact with her. Not over the next three weeks.

And when she started her period, she cried. Because she knew that he would come back. And she wanted him to. Because she was both upset and happy and she would never be able to sort those things out. Never be able to fully understand them.

She wiped her cheeks and sent him a text. And forced herself not to look at the phone.

She went downstairs and got herself some food.

Iliana looked at her with softness, and it irritated Maren.

"Are you well?"

"Just fine."

She went back to her room and was about to give in and check her texts when her phone rang.

It was her sister, Jessie. She'd been asking after how everything was, and Maren had been putting her off. And putting off the little detail that she had acquired herself a husband.

She sighed and answered the phone. "Hello."

"How are things, my princess?" Jessie asked.

"Princessy. How are you?"

"The size of a literal house. But Ewan is making sure all is well. He is a very accomplished foot masseuse."

"How nice for you," she said, feeling bitter and crampy.

"Anything new at the Palace on the Rock?"

And she decided then and there that she was just going to say it.

"I've had quite a lot of sex," said Maren.

She was satisfied that her sister was silent on the other end of the phone.

"With my husband," she finished, dramatically.

"Maren! What are you talking about?"

"Oh, the husband came with the castle. He is incredibly hot. And the decision to begin making a baby with him was quite easy. Though, we have not succeeded yet."

"You're going to have to back up."

So she told him all about Acastus and everything pertaining to the paperwork.

"You're joking," she said.

"I'm not," she said. "But he is not... Emotionally available. Which is fine. It's just that now he's away he's completely away and not in contact with me at all, and I sort of find it mean. Given that I gave him my virginity and everything."

"Oh, Maren," said Jessie. "You were so self-righteous with me. And I can't help but feel that you deserve this a little bit."

"That's very mean, Jessie," admitted Maren. "I'm fragile."

"I know. But you were not anything but meddlesome when it came to me and Ewan so I find that this is deserved. I'm sorry, darling."

"I don't think you are," said Maren, feeling hard done by.

"Well, I am. It's just that I also think it proves that you're human like I am. And maybe you can have a little bit more sympathy for me. I couldn't resist him."

Now she understood that, that was for sure.

"Gorgeous men are a pox. A scourge." Her phone buzzed. "He just texted me."

"Put me on speakerphone and read the text," said Jessie.

"Oh, lovely. He's sending me dates for our next booty call."

"Tell him no. Tell him to get screwed."

"That is what he's trying to do."

"You know what I mean."

"I can't tell him no," said Maren. "We have an agreement."

Jessie sighed. "You don't want to tell him no."

"Fine," she said. "I don't want to tell him no."

And that was the crux of the problem. She had missed him while he was away. It had been as much of a pleasure as it had been a torment to have those memories. To wonder what he was thinking. To wonder if he thought of her at all. The memories of his hands on her body were so sweet, and so terrible. She didn't want to let them out of her mind. She wanted to cling to them. To turn them over.

She felt wounded, regardless of the fact that she knew exactly what this was supposed to be. In some ways, it was terrible that she had been so right about herself. And in other ways... She almost enjoyed the way that it hurt.

She was not going to tell Jessie that bit of information. It was a bit too intimate.

And she had a week to look forward to the return of her husband.

It pained her how much she anticipated it. How much she wanted him.

But this was a situation she found herself in, and so... Why not enjoy it? When they were through, she would have a baby on the other side. She wouldn't feel quite so lonely. She would be whole, in many ways, like she hadn't been since her own mother had gone.

This would be another chance, after all. At a mother/child relationship, though this time with her in control of the outcome. This time with her being there, for always.

It would be well.

It would be.

And in the meantime, she would have wonderful sex.

The memory burned bright. But no matter how vivid her memory, it couldn't replace the real thing. It was her first experience with that. With it being so profoundly true.

It was a little bit frightening.

But she wanted the pleasure too much to turn away from it now.

# CHAPTER EIGHT

WORK HAD BEEN nothing more than a hideous grind. He had been waiting—more than he would like to admit—to hear from Maren. And when he had, it was all he could do not to go to her immediately.

But he would wait. Wait until the prescribed time.

Though he found that he just wished to be in her presence. Which was a strange experience, he had to admit.

Finally, it was time.

He left Athens behind without a backward glance and found himself looking forward to being back at the Palace on the Rock. As his boat approached the dock, he marveled at that.

He had hated it here as a child. And now… Was it not the sign of his triumph? It was, he supposed. But… It was more than that. Right now, it was about her. Right now, it was about having her.

Acastus clenched his fists in anticipation as he disembarked the boat and began to approach the palace.

He wondered what mood he would find his wife in.

She had seemed short on words when she had informed him that she was not pregnant.

But then, what words did they need?

He fought back against that slightly.

Because they had shared a great many words between them, and he had enjoyed that aspect of their relationship. She was wonderful in bed. But she was more than that.

When he arrived, he tried to think of where he might find her.

He checked in the room that had the cushions, because he knew that she liked those. But he did not find her there.

He looked in her bedroom, but she was not there.

And for some reason, he knew. Just suddenly.

He went into the dining room, and there she was, with a glass of orange juice, a cup of coffee and a piece of toast.

"Turn away from me, husband, for this is an intimacy too far. You said you did not wish to have toast with me."

He took a step toward her, picked up the toast, and took a bite out of it.

She looked up at him with outrage.

"Well, there. We have shared toast now."

"That was *mine*."

"It is ours now. A gesture of romance on my part, I think you'll find."

"That was…"

"Are you playing games with me?"

She shook her head. "No games."

"It seems as if you are, little one. I should not like to think that you are attempting to freeze me out of your bed by using toast as a weapon."

"Is your masculinity not up to the threat of toast?"

"I think I made my feelings on toast quite clear."

"Yes. By *eating* it."

"Is that not how one usually expresses their feelings regarding breakfast foods?"

She sniffed. "I wouldn't know, Acastus."

"I have waited," he said.

"You have barely spoken to me."

"It is our agreement. No toast and orange juice. And we will see to our lives in the meantime. Here you have all this glorious freedom. What have you done with it?"

"I have read many books," she said. "I watched whatever TV I wanted. And when I lay in bed at night, I parted my legs and put my hand between them and I thought of you."

She stole the toast back and took a bite.

"Thanks," he growled.

And it was as if he had never been gone.

He hauled her out of her chair and picked her up, carrying her to the bedroom.

He had her stripped bare before him instantly.

She was his. His.

It had been terrible being away from her.

*Terrible.*

He blocked that out, or he tried to, the memory of how his chest felt like a cavern without her. But the problem was, he kept on hearing that word echo over and over again. He kept on thinking about the way his *life* had felt like a particularly empty cavern without her.

He had known her a matter of a week. And in the time in between they had barely spoken.

Yet his life did not feel normal without her.

It did not feel right.

He kissed her neck, down her lovely body, down between her thighs.

He was starving for her.

She came apart in his arms, and then she kissed her way down his chest, down to his shaft, taking him deep inside of her mouth.

He gripped her hair, guided her movements. Luxuriating in the feel of her. In her touch.

In the fact that he was the only man that she had ever done this for.

*Mine.*

He arched his hips upward, and gave himself over to the need rioting through him.

She lay back on the bed, smiling up at him when they were through. "Well. I'm not getting pregnant doing it that way."

He growled at her.

Coming over the top of her and kissing her mouth. Their pleasure mingled in that kiss, and he knew that it would not take long for him to be able to do exactly what it took to make her pregnant.

"Are you spoiling for a fight?"

"Or something."

"Why is it you think you can play games with me?" he asked.

"Should I fear you?"

"Many do."

"I suppose," she said, moving her hands down to his masculinity. "The people that fear you have not held the source of your vulnerability in their hand."

He went hard. "Does that feel vulnerable to you?"

"Would you like me to test it?"

He bit her on the shoulder, and she sighed.

It felt good to be back with her, though he did not quite understand why.

He had made the decision to walk away without saying anything. To keep entirely to their agreement, because it had been the right thing to do. And he had to do that. He had to be strong, he had to continue to carry the boulder up the mountain because if he did not...

Weakness was unacceptable. A lack of control was unacceptable.

It would make him his father and that could never be endured.

Now he was back with her, and violating his own thoughts on the matter.

And he realized that he was far too close to feelings.

He moved away from her, in spite of the fact that he was ready to possess her.

"I wish to remind you, exactly what this is," he said. "We have an agreement. I am not answerable to you. I suggest you get over your pique and get ready to receive me."

She frowned. "I *was* ready to receive you. And now you're being an ass."

"You must be ready for me even if I am an ass."

"I feel certain I don't have to be. Why is it that you feel you get to make proclamations?"

"I feel," he said, "that it is fine and just for me to hold you to the expectations of our agreement."

"I'm a broodmare and you're my stud?"

"Yes," he said. "We've had an easy time slipping into conversation. But I do not wish for you to have expectations that should not be there."

"Oh, so now you're worried that I'll fall in love with you."

"Not if you actually knew me. But I am worried that you might paint fantasies around the fact that you and I can laugh with one another for brief moments. That we might be able to find enjoyment in each other's arms. That is nothing real."

"Is it not?"

"No. I will never fall in love with you. I will never want this to be a real marriage. We will never sit together in a domestic fashion."

It was brutal, the way that he was pushing her away, and he knew it. And unfair. He had come in happy to see her, and he was pushing back against his own feelings more than hers.

He knew that.

And yet.

He was punishing her for the feelings that she created inside of him because he knew that they were untenable.

And by twisting the knife he was reminding himself. That he was his father's son, and that feelings were a prison of their own construction. And he would not fall into that trap.

"Get out."

"You don't want me to leave. You want me to take you. Admit it."

"Did you not hear me when I said I'm more than capable of pleasuring myself? Anyway. I already got mine."

"You want *this*," he said, cupping his hardness. "You and I both know it."

"Trip and fall into the sea," she shot back.

"You need to make a baby with me."

"I think I'll skip today."

"Suit yourself," he said, growling and walking from the room.

In a fury, he took care of his arousal on his own. So that it would be impossible for him to go back to her.

Except he found that impossible with Maren was not what it had previously been defined as.

He lay awake hard all night.

And he regretted the enmity between them.

Even though he should want it.

Maren was sulky and unhappy the next day, and she did not pursue any kind of interaction with him. If she talked to him, she'd only yell at him.

He was infuriated. But he was infuriating. So really, his fault.

He was being awful. Unreasonably so. It was as if she had gotten too close to his heart, and he had felt bound to pull away. Determined to be cruel to her so that she wouldn't get any ideas. Or perhaps so *he* wouldn't.

He was there in the castle, and it was one of her precious fertility days, and they never spoke.

They didn't make love.

And it was true the next day.

And that following day was even one of her most fertile days.

She felt wretched. Pulled apart.

She didn't know why a fake marriage should be quite so difficult. It shouldn't be.

It should be easy. They should be easy.

This uncertainty reminded her far too much of what it was like to grow up in her father's orbit. When he and her mother had still been together and they had taken strips off of each other all the time. She'd seen love that had looked like hate. She'd been the child who'd watched her soft mother cry and cry. She'd felt it echo in her bones and she'd not been able to do a thing to fix it. It had carved out a sadness in her own soul that had never gone away.

She'd been the child whose mother had to run away because of how things were. And perhaps because she'd felt her mother's pain...she'd understood even though it hurt.

This was different.

They weren't in love. So why wasn't it easy?

She had no idea why in the world it wasn't. Why they weren't.

*Because you do have feelings for him. Because when you speak to him you feel like maybe he understands you.*

She decided to call her sister.

"I am having a fight with my husband," she said.

"Me too," said Jessie happily. "I'm looking forward to the makeup sex."

"You and Ewan fight?"

"Oh, yes. Thrillingly. He is such a stubborn, hardheaded man, and all of his healing has done nothing to eliminate that hardheadedness, but I wouldn't want it gone. I like that he is difficult. And he likes that I am. We are extremely compatible that way. We like it in or out of bed."

"I don't."

Jessie sighed. "Of course you don't. What's the problem?"

"He came back and I was teasing him, and at first he seemed to find it charming. We had a very… Satisfying interaction, though not one that's going to get me pregnant. And then he got distant. Strange. Mean."

Jessie snickered. "Sounds like a man."

"And now we're not speaking, and I… I want him."

"So have him, Maren. You don't need to wait for him. You don't even need to wait to not be angry at him. You can have him while you're furious. Sometimes that's fun."

"But I'm… Afraid of it. Of the intensity of it all. You know how things were with Mom and Dad…"

"What does that have to do with him?"

"It could be like it was with them, if we let it."

"If you let it, I suppose, but you aren't them." But how did you become them? That was what Maren didn't know.

This wasn't what she'd signed up for. She'd wanted to make a baby, not get obsessed with an infuriating, unknowable man with a cold aura and a hot body.

"I think it's best if you embrace it," said Jessie. "I think the very marvelous thing about relationships like the one you're in with him is that they're not like anything else."

"I'm not supposed to be in a relationship with him."

"He's your lover. You've never had another lover. How many people on this earth would you want to be close to, make love to, even while you were angry with them?"

"So far only him."

"*Exactly.* So embrace it. Be with him. Be with him because you want him. Be with him because it's wonderful, and you want to make love with him. And don't worry about the rest. Because it's already sharp and spiky, isn't it? Dangerous."

"Well. Yes. That it is."

"Great. So please yourself. Take risks. See where it takes you."

She pondered that for a while, and then found herself going into her closet to choose an elaborate piece of lingerie.

She would have him. But she wouldn't let it be… It didn't have to be like her parents. She was too self-aware for that.

Because she wanted him. Yes, she was angry, and yes, it was difficult. She didn't understand why her feelings for him were so… Big. When in reality they barely knew each other. Except she couldn't escape from those moments where they had connected. Maybe the issue was she hadn't had friends growing up, and he was maybe the closest thing to one other than her sister. But they had complicated it with sex and need.

Whatever the issue, she liked him, and she missed him.

Even when she was furious at him.

But she could make this work. She knew that it wasn't love. She *liked* him. When she didn't want to eviscerate him with her teeth. She wanted him. It could be straightforward if she wanted it to be.

She put on an entirely see-through lavender chiffon gown that went all the way to the floor, but showed the silhouette of her body beneath.

And with boldness, she walked the short distance down the corridor to his room.

She knocked. And it was like that first night. When she had come in and found him about to have a drink. Shirtless and barefoot and sexy.

"You are quite routine oriented," she said. "And perhaps I am too."

"What are you here for?"

"You."

"You want a baby that badly?"

"I want *you* that badly. I'm furious at you. You're impossible and difficult. But I want you. I will be very disappointed if you go away tomorrow without me having you." He moved to her, his eyes hard, his expression stern. He gripped her chin, held her fast as he looked into her eyes. "Finally," he said, and then he leaned in and kissed her. Hard and deep.

And she was a prisoner to it.

In that moment, she was held captive by her desire for him.

Domination. Submission. Strength. Weakness. She was all of it.

She kissed him like it was the only thing. Like there was an endless sea of kissing to swim through, and she would never find the end of it. Never find the depths.

She kissed him, and she was made new.

Suddenly all of the anger that she'd been sitting in the last few days seemed shallow.

Clearly, he had experienced a life like hers. Complex facets of tragedy and hope and family and disappointment.

So of course he felt like pushing away from whatever this was between them. She could understand the impulse.

But maybe it was up to her to persist.

To what end?

Maybe just this. Right now, maybe just this. Because the connection that she felt with him was profound, and felt as if it could not be accidental. She didn't want it to be.

With shocking strength and swiftness he pushed her up against the wall, captured her wrists and pushed them up above her head. She gasped.

And she allowed him to take the lead.

His movements were ferocious, and hungry. And she reveled in them.

He stripped the gown off of her body, leaving her naked before him.

Then he wrapped his hand around her thigh and lifted it up over his hip, grinding his cloth-covered arousal against where she was wet and aching for him.

She wanted him. Just like this.

Her hands were fast and furious on his belt as she freed him and positioned him at the entrance to her body, then he pinned her against the wall as he took possession of her.

He thrust hard into her, grunting like an animal, and she loved it.

The lack of control between them.

If she could capture and hold on to each and every moment of this she would count herself lucky, not cursed.

Maybe she was a cliché. The sad virgin who was catching feelings for the first man she'd ever been with.

But he was also her husband.

And she was also her.

Someone who had been kept separate from others for so much of her life, and now she had found a brilliant and blinding connection that surpassed anything else she had ever known.

There was nothing cliché about her. Because no one else was really like her.

Her sister, Jessie came the closest, but Maren was Maren.

And in this moment, Acastus was Acastus. And he was the only man, the only thing, who could ever satisfy her.

Their race toward the climax was quick, their peak triumphant. And when they collapsed into the bed together, they were both spent and exhausted, but unwilling to release their hold on each other.

He turned to her many times that night, and she willed herself not to fall asleep, because she didn't want to miss it if he decided to get up and leave.

But eventually sleep claimed her, and in the morning he was gone.

She didn't have to search the whole castle to know that he had left.

Again.

She sent him a text, and she knew that he wasn't going to respond.

It disappointed her anyway.

# CHAPTER NINE

THE WEATHER TURNED colder as August became September, and Maren missed her period.

She wanted to mourn, in a strange way. Because that meant that he wouldn't come see her this month.

Then she cleared her head.

She was having a baby. One time. They had been together one time during that week, and it had been a lost and furious sort of night. How had she managed to conceive?

It didn't matter how, just that she had.

She was awash in so many feelings. A rainbow of them. So strong she could nearly see them wrap around her like a glowing aura. Fear, anguish, joy, excitement, worry, anxiety, elation. Opposites and shades of the same tone. All brilliant and a bit too much. It took her breath away. She had to sit quietly with it, for a while, letting all bloom within her like a garden.

She didn't tell him. Not the first day.

But she texted him the second day.

I'm pregnant.

Good.

That was his only response. No indication on when she would see him again.

So Maren put her phone away, and determined not to obsess about it. Not to obsess about him.

She called Jessie and told her the news—from a different number, one that he didn't have.

Jessie was pleased for her, but also nearing giving birth herself, so couldn't make the trip out to see her.

"After your baby is born," she said. "But how nice that the cousins will be so close in age."

It was about the only thing that made her happy right then.

The only thing that made her feel like things were going to be okay.

And then her morning sickness started. Furiously. September rolled into October, and she was still ill. She took classes on her computer, business and marketing and all manner of things to keep her brain busy. And felt ill.

November was art classes and being sicker.

And then finally December, and she was round and angry and thought of Acastus far more than she would like.

It had been months. She shouldn't care. And she

did. So much it hurt. She waffled between outrage, vomit and sadness.

She got tired and settled on sadness the first week of the month.

She found herself lying in bed most days, feeling miserable.

Her feelings had always been far too big and volatile. She hated them. She hated the way they felt close to her parents and their drama. She hated the way she couldn't imagine this baby. That she'd been putting off a doctor's appointment because she was too afraid to deal with it all.

She escaped into her mind palace, perhaps too deeply. Trying to find comforting, familiar images. Old feelings of happiness, images of old picture books, or favorite scenes in childhood cartoons.

She was a princess, and wholly lost in what that was even supposed to mean.

Her life had been upended entirely when she found out that she was married to Acastus, and she had become obsessed with him. She had forgotten why she was here. She had forgotten that initially what she wanted was a baby.

And now her pregnancy was making her utterly physically miserable.

While she sat around missing a man who likely never thought of her.

She wept a lot.

It was December, and she had such fantasies of what she was going to do for Christmas.

And now she didn't have the energy to do it.

She stopped leaving her bedroom.

She would just lie there and read, and drink tea.

She was hard-pressed to find anything she wanted to eat.

She forgot why she was here. She forgot why the castle mattered.

She wished that she had simply walked away from him rather than taking him up on any of this, because here she was grappling with the consequences while he…

She turned over in bed and put her pillow over her head. She wasn't going to think about him.

She wasn't.

And he would never know about her despair. And that was how it needed to be.


When he received the call from Iliana he was incensed.

"She is ill?"

"Yes, Your Highness, she never gets out of bed. She has sunk into a terrible melancholy."

"Why has no one reached out to me before? Why have you not called the physician?"

"She did not wish for us to call anyone. She wished to handle it all on her own. She's very stubborn. But she's gotten worse this month and I can no longer bear it."

He was familiar with her stubbornness.

"I will be there soon."

He had avoided her. And he knew it was wrong of him.

His phone rang again, and it was his mother.

"Acastus," she said. "Will you be joining me in Palermo for Christmas?"

"Why don't you come to the palace, Mother?"

"I'm not sure that I can stand going there."

His heart froze. "I thought that you wanted it?"

He knew she did. She'd been unhappy forever because of the lack of it and now she didn't wish to... claim that happiness?

"I'm deeply appreciative that with your marriage to the Princess I am now Queen Mother." Thanks to the unconventional rules of the very strange, tiny country that was a rock in the middle of the sea. One he'd fought for. One he'd made it his life's work to obtain for her. "And that you will make me a grandmother, what a legacy. I'll be able to tell everyone. But why should I leave my shiny life with all of my friends? I have nothing but atrocious memories associated with that place. With that country life..."

He'd built that glittering life for her, and she'd been clear then it hadn't been enough. He'd carved it out from blank stone from nothing, his blood and his sweat in the foundation, and yet it had never been enough then.

So he'd gone on. To make sure the promise of her being royalty was fulfilled, and now she was acting as if that was only ever a trinket she was after? Like a new diamond to show off to her friends? When she had acted for all this time as if it was the air she breathed?

He had done this for her. And the way she took only the part that was easiest and most convenient for her galled him even as he made excuses.

He took a breath and tried to reason this out. Tried to find control.

She had been unhappy for so many years. If Palermo made her happy, why should she go to the palace?

There was no point getting mad at his mother. Not ever. She was far too fragile, she could never withstand the weight of his anger, and it only upset both of them in the end.

"Whatever suits you best, Mother, but I'm going to have to spend my Christmas there."

"Why?"

"Because I must be with my wife."

"Don't tell me you've gone and fallen for her. You don't wish to be tied to that place. Tied to one person."

"I have not," he said. "She is ill. Her pregnancy... I must go to her."

"You always did do a very good job of taking on responsibility," she said.

And *that* pleased him.

That was a reminder of who he was. What he was.

He was a man who did not let those in his charge twist in the wind.

He did not let them sink into unhappiness. He was not his father. And he never would be.

He would take care of Maren because it was the right thing to do, and then he would return to his life in Athens.

When he got to the palace, it was dark.

He didn't know what he had expected... Yes he did. He'd expected the place to be all lit up for Christmas. Because Maren had spoken of that, with shining eyes. Of everything she'd wanted to do, and she hadn't done it yet.

He found Iliana, and stopped her in the hallway. "Ready the palace for Christmas," he said.

"Yes sir but..."

"Top to bottom. Every room. I wish for it to be unquestionably bright in here. It must be a Christmas fit for a princess."

"Yes sir."

"Is she in her room?"

"Yes. As she ever is."

"Then I will go to her. And while I am with her, find all of the decoration she had ordered and make this place a fantasy for her."

He made his way up the stairs, and he went into her bedroom without knocking.

He was surprised to see her lying there, so pale and small in the center of the massive bed.

"Maren."

"And you must be the Ghost of Christmas Past." She shook her head. "Because you certainly aren't actually here."

She had staff. An entire staff of people and none of them could be moved to care for her better than this? He was appalled. And he shoved aside any recriminations he had for himself.

He had done exactly as he had told her he would do. Nothing more, nothing less. He did not make promises that he did not fulfill.

Her staff, on the other hand, was clearly not caring for her as they ought to.

"You are not well," he said.

"No indeed," she commented. "I am not. How astute of you to observe."

"It is all well with the baby?"

"As far as I know. I was told there was no reason to see a doctor until—"

"Unacceptable."

He opened the door and thundered out into the corridor. "Iliana," he barked. "Contact a physician for my wife."

"The Princess has said…"

"I am in residence now. I will decide what is to be done." He shut the door and turned back to the bed.

"This place is mine," said Maren angrily. "You are only here because of our marriage. I'm the one that won a castle."

He felt like he could hear the foot stomp embedded in her voice.

"And I'm the one that earned a billion dollars and has real power outside of this place. Do you not understand?" He thundered toward the bed. "I am the one who has real consequence here. I am the one. You are carrying my child, and you will do what needs to be done to keep that child safe."

He hated seeing her pale. He hated seeing her diminished. He could not find it in him to say that. So he railed about the pregnancy because it was what they were. It was why he was here. At least that was what they had agreed upon.

"I'm surviving," she said.

"This is not survival. Have you really lain down in your bed because of my absence?" He had said it largely to make her angry. To test her.

It worked.

She sat up in bed, red spots of color appearing on her cheeks. "I feel sick. I'm hormonal and I feel depressed. Your absence has nothing to do with anything." She lifted her hands and hit the top of the comforter. "I spent twenty-two years without you in my life, and I would happily spend twenty-two more without you. Except the twenty-two on the other side of this will be me caring for a child that we created together. And that is probably the most involvement that we will have with one another. Do you honestly think I'm such a giant baby that I took to my bed because you weren't here? That I'm depressed without your penis? It's *morning sickness*."

"It seems a damn sight more than that. When I tried to get a hold of you—"

"I'm in contact with my sister. All the time. I'm not in contact with you because I put that phone away. There was no reason to sit by it. Tell me, until recently did you try to contact me once?"

"No…"

She was like a little teapot now, sputtering fury as the fire beneath her raged. "Does it bother you, Acastus, that actually I have been thinking of myself since I found out that I was pregnant with my child? Does it bother you that I did not sit by the phone and wait? I think that you *want* me to be in love with you."

Her eyes gleamed with triumph, and he was shocked to find her words hooked into something inside him. And pulled tight.

He shook his head, the denial coming from deep within him. "I don't. I don't want love. Not yours, not anyone's."

"*Yes*. Sure. So you've said. Because of something

to do with your mother. I'm sure the therapist would have a lot to say about that."

"I don't need a therapist to say anything about it. I have my mother to communicate with still. She is fragile. She always has been. The way that she loved my father was a prison. She was stuck with him, in spite of the fact that he could fulfill none of his promises to her."

"She was unhappy," said Maren. "That much is clear. You know that she was unhappy, because she told you. Why was she unhappy?"

"Because we worked here," he said. "Imagine it as it was then. Stavros, his wife and daughter, and my family. Working in clear servitude to them. My father practically licking his boots to beg for me to be allowed to marry his daughter. My father clinging to that promise because he had told my mother she'd have a title, when he could have gone away and provided better for us. But he knew it was all he was worth and so we remained. In misery. And Stavros continually moved the bar. We simply had to complete this task or that. Serve another year, and then her hand would be granted. And then… And then I stole from him."

He watched Maren's face carefully as he began to tell the story. "There was something my mother wanted desperately and she felt we were owed because of all the time Stavros tarried with his promises." He looked at the wall behind her now, unable to look at her. "For my sins, I was beaten. Thrown in the dungeon. His daughter came to tell me herself that she would never marry me. She said I was nothing. Nothing but a servant. Little better than a slave. A poor boy who would never amount to anything, and whom she would never marry.

"He made it known that I ruined everything. I stole the chance for my family to have this place. My father died after that. His heart gave out. After years of him keeping us in poverty waiting on unfulfilled promises, he had the temerity to die, not to fight. Not for me, not for my mother, not for anyone." His heart thundered erratically as he recounted the story. It always did.

It always got to him.

It always made him feel like a failure.

He could remember his mother saying as much in her despair. Because this had been so important to her. It had been.

And now it was not?

He pushed that to the side.

It was all his father's fault.

He'd put them in the position where they were desperate. And then had the nerve to leave them by dying.

To leave them as lowly as they ever had been. To leave them with nothing.

"It was up to me. It was up to me to save us. To

fix this. To redeem all of it for my mother. For her great sacrifice. The way that she stayed with him."

"Why did she stay with him?"

"Because she loved him," he said.

"You say that. You continue to say that. But if she was miserable, and if she was miserable because of what they didn't have, then how much could she have loved him? Or did she just want to be royalty?"

"You sacrificed everything to be a princess. Your freedom. You signed yourself over to me."

"Yes. I did."

"How can you act as if it's not a compelling piece of bait?"

"I'm not. I'm not acting as if it's not compelling at all. But I've never pretended to love you."

"And yet you have wilted in my absence."

"Again!" she nearly shrieked. "*I'm pregnant.* And we have gone in a circle. Why is it that you wish to believe that love is a cage? Were you simply looking for confirmation?"

"Because it holds you to another person when good sense would have dictated you leave long ago."

She looked so angry it would have been funny— so fluffy as she was—f the anger was not clearly so real. "I think the pregnancy is a cage."

"Do you not want the baby?"

Right in that moment he felt like throwing the offer out there. A challenge. An offer for her to cut ties with him and with all of this. What if they decided to simply…not do this? To walk away from it and each other.

"No," she said quickly. "I want the baby."

His breath caught. He hadn't realized that he had been afraid of her answer.

"I just don't feel well." She sounded less angry now. Mostly tired. "You're the one catastrophizing it." She laughed. "Or even worse, making it somehow about me being in love with you."

If he could take back one thing he'd said, it would be the implication she loved him. It felt somehow far too exposing.

"You need to arise. And eat," he said.

"I'm not feeling very well," she said.

"And you think you'll feel well if you continue to lie here? At least go into your study. Sit there. Have a change of scenery."

"You don't get to tell me what to do."

"You will have a bath." He'd decided it then, and he was certain he was right. She looked drab and gray in pallor. She needed to warm herself. He went to the bed and picked her up.

She howled, and he carried her straight through her closet and into the bathroom.

"I do not need to stay. But I will be nearby if you need help. Bathe. Put on something new, and I will meet you in your study."

And he turned and left her there, disliking the tangle of feeling in his chest. Disliking everything.

Everything about this, and everything about the words that she had lobbed at him.

Of course he didn't want her to love him. He could think of nothing worse. The problem was, he worried she might, because it looked so like the love his mother had suffered at the hands of his father.

She had loved him, and he had not seen to her needs.

Would Maren be like that? Would she need to lean on their child because he wasn't here?

It wasn't his mother's fault.

And by extension it could not be Maren's fault if he was absentee and he created the situation.

He was going to have to rethink. Everything.

What a fool he'd been.

He had been in charge of his own destiny from the time he'd been old enough to seize control.

He had believed that it meant something. He had believed that it meant he would be in control always. He had thought it would be the easiest thing in the world and yet he had not counted on her.

Yes, things would change.

He would see to it.

# CHAPTER TEN

MAREN WAS FULMINATING the entire time she took her bath. She had to stop scrubbing because she was doing it so angrily it was leaving red marks.

She had no idea what he was thinking. Coming in here and taking charge, carrying her into the bathroom. As if he knew what she wanted.

As if he knew what she needed.

She did end up taking a bath, though.

And she enjoyed it. Felt like probably it was a good thing that she had paused to do something to take care of herself. She was angry at him. For coming in and accusing her of sinking into despair because of him. When he was exactly as he had promised to be, and she really didn't even know him.

It was a pity that it was so easy for her to like him. A pity that when they spoke they seemed to have so much in common. And even worse that when he touched her they had so much chemistry. Because when it came to the specific amount of time that they had actually known one another, it was ludicrous to suggest that she might have feelings for him.

But sometimes it felt like the connection she had to him transcended sanity.

It was deeply problematic.

Deeply.

He was tangled up about emotion, she could see that. And she wasn't really any better. They were both a disaster, and she was going to have a baby in a few months' time, so she couldn't afford to be disastrous.

She thought of her mother. She had gotten herself tangled up with the wrong man, and she hadn't been able to...

She'd had to get away. Maren understood that. She didn't judge her mother. She didn't. She understood that her mother had had to take care of herself. The thing with their father was toxic and horrible, and her mother had wept all the time. He'd never hurt her physically but he wasn't a safe man. Her mother had loved a dangerous man far too much and she'd had to leave.

If she had taken Jessie and Maren with her she might've been pursued.

Maren understood that. But it was also why she truly believed that a person could not afford to get sidetracked. Her mother had been in love with her father, and that was why she had made a decision and linked herself to someone dangerous.

She did not believe that Acastus was dangerous. She just had a feeling. And maybe it was foolish to put so much stock in her feelings. Given all that she knew and didn't know about men. But she had to put her trust in something, right? If she didn't, then she would simply be a tragic human being. She did trust that he wouldn't hurt her. But she also knew that she did need to keep herself from getting tangled up. And unfortunately there was a little bit of truth to the fact that she had taken to her bed because she was upset about him. About the leaving and the fact it was a pattern in her life she couldn't escape.

This was not the first time she'd been bruised, that was the problem.

It was this persistent pressing where she was already injured. Again and again.

She had to stop. She had to keep her head on straight. He was everything that he had promised her. He was not in love with her, just as he had said he wouldn't be.

That was not a failure on his part.

She had asked for him to keep distance. She should be glad that he had honored that promise. She should be.

And she needed to get a hold of herself. It was a hard wake-up call, his return. The way that he had responded to her.

It had drawn a stark line beneath just how much she had let herself get swallowed up in melancholy.

She had been in touch with Jessie. Frequently.

Her sister had been concerned. But Jessie's pregnancy hadn't been as difficult as Maren's.

Maren was very sick. Feelings notwithstanding. And she did think that her hormones had kicked her specifically in the rear.

She went into her closet, and selected a dress. Red and glittery, and far over-the-top for a midmorning visit with her estranged husband.

Was he even estranged? When everything that had occurred between them had been exactly as planned. It was just her feelings. And this was the problem. She just had a lot of feelings.

She was trying to do something about them. But the truth was, she was going to become a mother. And it was bringing up a lot of things.

Things from her past.

But it should serve as a reminder.

A very timely one.

She put on some red lipstick and a bit of gold eyeshadow, and some blush so that she didn't quite look like the specter of death she felt.

And then she walked out into…

A flurry of activity. There were ladders up in the corridor, and staff hanging greenery from the rafters. There were crimson bows and reeds going up in three-foot intervals with the garlands.

There was Christmas music playing. Being piped

into speakers that were installed up at the top of the walls. It was a very merry explosion.

"What's happening?" she asked.

"Princess," said one of the men. "It's so good to see you up."

"Thank you," she said. "What's going on?"

"The Prince has demanded that we ready the castle for Christmas."

She'd wanted that. A Christmas in this castle. She'd told him so.

They'd never had Christmas growing up.

And she had tried to establish little traditions with Jessie, but Jessie really wasn't sentimental about that. Maren had always felt like she wanted to be sentimental, and had never been allowed to.

And she'd been so sick that she hadn't gotten around to doing the Christmas that she wanted.

And here it was. Going up all around her at Acastus's request.

"How… Beautiful."

She walked slowly through all the chaos, her eyes widening.

And by the time she got to her sitting room, she was absolutely stunned.

There was a massive Christmas tree in the sitting room. The fire was roaring, and the tree was twinkling with white lights and brilliant decorations.

"This…oh, my…" she said.

And there he was. Wearing a dark suit, looking

as stunning as ever. He was not lounging. He was standing by the fire, his hands in his pockets.

"Is that suit jacket a bit warm?"

"Don't worry about me. You are…up."

His dark gaze swept over her.

She found herself blushing.

Her pregnancy was beginning to show, and she hadn't felt much about that at all until right at this moment. When he looked at her with hungry eyes that seemed satisfied by the change in her figure.

"A little bit of scrubbing has done you well," he said.

"Well, thank you," she said, waspishly.

"I am having a tray of food brought in."

"You know I like food," she said cautiously.

"I do know that."

"You know you give yourself far too much credit," she said, because she had been roiling with these thoughts and feelings and she felt that he ought to as well. "The idea of becoming a mother is bringing up a lot of my own childhood issues. I should think that every person faced with impending parenthood has a thought or two about how it links to the way they were raised. You're right. Love is a cage. My mother experienced that. And she escaped the cage. But she left us in it."

"What do you mean?"

"My mother was beautiful." She felt herself softening even as she thought of her mother now. "She had a closet full of beautiful clothes. She was always dressed up. I have her hair. She used to let me play with her makeup and her jewelry. She said that I was beautiful. She said that I was a princess. And I believed her. She was the best part of my life, and when I close my eyes and call up those memories I can still see her. So clearly."

"You said you have an eidetic memory," he said. "So that means that you have perfect recall of that time spent with your mother."

"Yes. And equally of the time spent with my father. My sister... I know she protected me from much of it. She's very strong. She had a head for numbers, and while I'm good with them too—it's a side effect of the memory—Jessie is a little bit of a genius. And she flung herself in front of me in a way that no one else did. She had something to do, though. And I just felt sad that our mother was gone. I have always felt sad about that. I just wish... I wish that she wasn't gone. And I miss her. I never want to be in a position where whatever relationship I have with you impacts the way that I parent our child."

He straightened abruptly. "It is strange that you would say that, because I was just thinking the same thing. I... My father was absent. He was focused on serving here at the palace. He was almost awash in his own self-pity over the fact that he did not achieve what he wanted in the time frame he wanted it. My mother was lonely. I cooked for her. I was her listening ear. It is not her fault, of course. He abandoned her to that fate."

"That sounds like an incredibly intense amount of pressure to put on a boy," she commented.

"I did not mind. I have never minded stepping up and being the man that my father refused to be. I have always accepted that I needed to be the one."

He turned and faced the fire again, and she felt an intense squeeze in her chest. Her own mother had abandoned her. His had… Had taken from him. She could see that. Love was a cage, but for who? Was he in a cage of having to care for his mother?

She didn't want that either. And look at the way that she was behaving. The way that she had allowed herself to get so… Bogged down.

"I will be there for our child. Always. I promise. I would never leave," she said.

"And I will not put you in a position where you must lean on the child."

"I don't blame my mother," she said.

"Neither do I," he returned.

And yet the air seemed filled with heavy feeling, and things that they could not say. His own unhappiness, the weight of it, of all that he'd carried for so long bore down on her. And she had to wonder if anyone had ever felt what he did.

She wondered if even he felt it. Or if he simply shrugged like Atlas, and carried on, holding an insurmountable weight.

She found she wanted to help him carry it. But she might have to set down some of what she was carrying to do it and that just seemed…well, it didn't seem possible.

So she tried to push past it, tried to breathe past it. Even thought it was hard.

"I really just haven't been feeling well. But I did notice in the last few days that I was beginning to feel better."

"The doctor will be here to visit you. To look you over."

"But I told you I shouldn't need to see anyone…"

"I feel that I would be remiss if you were not wholly cared for and looked over. You are having my baby. And you need to be cared for."

"I did make sure that I wasn't missing out on any appointments. I haven't had any bleeding or anything abnormal. I'm not concerned."

"But I am."

"Yes. And now you're here so you're taking over."

"We are at an impasse. I have decided that our original agreement is untenable. I fear that it will put our child in the same position that I was in. And it will make me my father. And of all the things that I refuse, that is the one that I refuse the most deeply. I am not my father."

"Well, I am not my mother. And I will not…" She stopped herself. Her heart felt sore. She loved her mother.

She didn't tend to blame her mother for what had happened. Her father had been a criminal.

And yet... And yet she could not say that she wanted to be like her mother. In some way she did want to be. If she had a daughter, she wanted to share in her love of soft things. Jewelry and makeup. If she had a son, she wanted to sit and talk with him.

She wanted to make her child feel special. She wanted to be able to say you are a prince or princess. And mean it. She had made this life for them.

And those things, those assurances, the way that her mom had made her feel special, that was real.

But at the same time, she wished to never have her child feel abandoned. Ever. "My mother was good to me."

"She hurt you," he said.

She shook her head. "My father hurt me. It was only that... I guess sometimes it's impossible not to think that perhaps I wasn't important enough."

It was like she had reached down inside of herself and pulled out her deepest, most concealed fear. Like she had shone a flashlight on something that shamed her. She didn't want to think badly of her mother. She had been the kindest person other than her sister ever in her life. She was the source of so many good memories. So many.

And when that realization, that feeling, opened up the door on a different memory, one that she kept behind the tallest, thickest door in the mind palace, she couldn't look away.

The day she had discovered her mother gone. All the beautiful clothes gone with her. All of her jewelry.

And the way she had cried in the emptiness.

The way she had felt all the emptiness in that room fill her up.

The way she had been certain she would never be happy again.

A child abandoned and left in this harsh world.

"I just don't understand why she couldn't take me with her."

"She should have," he said.

"It would've put us in danger."

"Didn't leaving you put you in danger?"

His words were harsh and stark, and they twisted something deep inside of her.

She wondered if Jessie felt that way, but never said it because Maren loved their mother so much.

Jessie didn't talk about their mother. Not in the same way Maren did.

Not often.

Was she the only one that didn't see this?

She felt beset.

In pain.

"We lived. We survived. We…"

"So did I," he said. "So did my mother."

"You blame your father for all of your unhappiness. Well, so do I. If my father hadn't chosen to be a criminal…"

"Your mother chose your father."

"Well, at least I have the very real truth that I didn't choose you."

His lip curled. "Indeed."

"But the same could be said for your mother anyway."

"He bait and switched. He promised her a lifestyle that he could not provide."

"But did he behave like a different man? Was it simply that the man wasn't enough if he didn't come with money?"

"You don't know what you're speaking about."

"I know well enough," she said. "I know well enough. What you're talking about is love."

"And you know what love is?"

She wanted to say that she did. But…

"I don't know. I love my sister. She loves me. She has protected me. And I did my best to return the favor when she needed it. I believe that her husband loves her. And she loves him. But they speak in a language that I don't understand, and looking at them is painful. I do know what love is. I have only ever felt it in the smallest of ways. But I did feel it when I was with my mother. I did."

"You will love your child," he said. "You have no need to worry about that."

"I've never worried about that. Do you?"

"I'm not worried about it. What is love, anyway? What is it but care? My father failed to demonstrate his love for his family. Whatever he said he felt, how could it ever be true? When he left us to fend for ourselves. When he left his son to serve time in a dungeon."

She looked at him. "What did you steal?"

He looked down. "Jewels. For my mother."

"Jewels. That's… Incredibly high value."

"Yes it was," he said. "It was a foolish thing to do, and not something she asked of me."

Except it was far too easy for her to imagine based on the clues that he had given her about his mother. She was fragile. She longed for fine things. His father wouldn't provide them. And so he had done what any bold teenage boy might do.

"Was your mother angry? When you lost that marriage bargain."

He nodded. "Yes. She was very angry. She was really angry at my father."

"I think it sounds like your mother was miserable. I think she's one of those people, she's unhappy and she makes it about everyone else around her. It was your father's fault, and it was your job to fix it."

She could see so clearly that his mother had taken advantage of him. And it made her wonder what he was seeing so clearly with her.

It was like they were both holding pet trauma to

their chest, and they didn't want to release their control over their own perception of that trauma.

Seemed fair, really. Their trauma had been with them a lot longer than each other had. Why should she tear herself open for him? Why should she respond to what he was saying?

Still. It made her want to talk to Jessie. Ask her what she was thinking about in regards to motherhood, and their mother, and all the things really.

"Should a son not work to bring happiness to his mother's life?"

"I suppose, Acastus. Hard to know, since I'm not a son and my mother left me. But I do think maybe there's a difference. I think a mother should take joy in her son. Because he is. Because he's there. And anything he does should be admired and appreciated, I suppose, but you should not be…treated as if her tears are a problem for you to solve."

"You don't know what you're talking about."

Her chest ached. "Unfortunately, I do. I feel it. I feel how heavy this is for you, and the way you describe her…makes sense to me. I can see it. I can see exactly what kind of person she is, and what she did to you isn't fair."

He said nothing to that. He simple stared at the wall, his breath heavy, his jaw set.

She decided to change the subject.

"Why did you have them decorate for Christmas?"

"You said that you wanted it."

"I did. I do. But it seems… Well, it seems out of character in terms of being thoughtful."

"Did I not just put you in a warm bath?"

"You set me down in the bathroom and demanded I draw my own bath."

"I would've been perfectly happy to strip you naked and put you in the bath myself, however, I suspected that it would not be well received. All things considered."

"Specifically that we had an agreement to have sex only to conceive?"

"Seeing you naked is not sex."

"With the two of us has it ever not been?"

Her tongue tingled at the intimate sentence. *With us.*

It spoke of the history that stretched back more than just the last six months, but it felt like so much more. It was days out of all that time. But she had been naked with him, and they had confided in one another.

And now there was all this… Acreage of hurt between them. All of this nonsense. Everything that they were.

"When will the doctor be here?"

"In an hour or so."

"Fantastic. I can be examined while being surrounded by Christmas cheer."

"And I will be there. There is something that you must understand. Things have changed as far as I'm concerned. I must be a more involved father than I originally intended."

She looked at him. And she felt a deep tension rising up inside of her, because she was afraid of that. Afraid of what it would do to her. And the simple truth was, she didn't want for the relationship with her child to become tangled because of him. Because of her feelings for him.

"If you wish to be an involved father I will not stop you, but you and I must have very clear ground rules. Our marriage has to be in name only. From here on."

"If that's what you wish."

"It's what must be."

She was tangled up in him already. That was the truth of it. She had already allowed his absence to wound her.

She had already bent herself into impossible shapes, she had already been tragic and lost without him.

She had to maintain distance and sanity.

Because she could see…

If he broke her heart, if she needed to get away from him…

No. She would never do that to a child, but she would simply make sure…

She would make sure.

"That's how it has to be," she reiterated. "That is how it will be."

A large tray of food was brought in then, and his eyes flickered over it, and then to her. "Eat your food. The doctor will be here shortly, and you will need your strength."

She would like to argue with him. Coming in here and being so autocratic, but the truth was... The staff worked for her, and they listened to her when she said that she didn't need to be taken care of. They listened to her when she said that she didn't need encouragement to get out of bed.

She had, clearly.

She needed someone who wouldn't just listen to her.

That was how Jessie had always been.

Maren would say something in a huff, and Jessie would challenge her.

Acastus challenged her.

She didn't want to need him. It was inconvenient. But he was here.

Perhaps she could make that be all that mattered.

Perhaps she could remind herself that it was more of the family dynamic. Like her sister.

Maybe they could be like family. Maybe she could do something about the endless pain in her chest when she thought of him.

Maybe there was a way to fix all of this. Just maybe.

Keeping their marriage in name only was a start. An important one.

And she was bound and determined to stick to it.

# CHAPTER ELEVEN

EVEN AFTER COMING and finding her ill everything felt theoretical until the doctor arrived. With official medical equipment and credentials and not a small amount of concern.

"You do look a bit poorly," the doctor said.

And it made Acastus angry, because who was this person to come in and say that Maren looked poorly, as if it was an indictment of her and the way she had taken care of herself? Or the way that he had taken care of her.

"She has been unwell," he said to the doctor.

"So I gather," the doctor said.

In the bedroom, there was medical equipment set up. He didn't know what any of it was, and he hated that feeling. Of being out of his depth. Of not understanding. It reminded him of being a child. It was something that he had gone out of his way not to experience as an adult.

He had become powerful. He had become the one

with money. The one with the power to dangle a sword over someone's head like the blade of Damocles. He didn't. He chose not to. But he also never allowed himself to be in situations where he might feel that way again. And suddenly his whole life had careened out of his reach.

Suddenly, everything seemed mysterious. Seemed like something he could not grasp hold of.

He didn't like it.

To say the least.

He also didn't like it when Maren stripped down to nothing, then put on a gown that tied at the back, and seemed fragile beneath the sheet. When her beauty became something clinical, and he felt as if she was not being touched with the reverence that she ought to be. And perhaps it made no sense, but he did not care.

It made sense to him.

He felt like if anyone was going to put their hands on her it should be in the context of the idea that she was the most beautiful creature in the world.

Even if he was not allowed to put his hands on her at all.

His focus was on her face, and it took him a moment to realize that the doctor was performing an ultrasound.

And that the noise that filled the room was the sound of the baby's heartbeat.

His own heart slammed against his rib cage in response, when he did realize.

It was… It was miraculous in a way that he had never thought before. In his mind this idea of having a child had been about legacy.

He had not thought about the magnitude of it. That he and Maren coming together, touching, kissing, being intimate with one another, had created this heartbeat.

That it would grow into a child, who would become a man or woman in their own right, independent of their parents with their own desires, hopes and fears. Their own scars from their childhood.

It suddenly felt impossibly high stakes.

How could he know what the right things were? How could he figure out how to minimize damage? Because didn't parents always cause damage?

So how could he do his very best to not, especially when he didn't even understand…

He had no connections. He had his mother. He had his money. He had business associates. And there was Maren.

He had felt something upon his first meeting with her. And it had only increased in the time they had spent together. It was, he realized then, their loneliness that allowed them to speak. That allowed them that connection. But loneliness was not something they could pass on to a child. It was no real legacy.

There had to be something more. Something different.

And he did not know how to find it. And that heartbeat, pounding through him, echoing his own... That heartbeat was the most terrifying sound he'd ever heard in his life.

And then he heard another.

"Is that hers?" he asked.

"No," the doctor said, his eyes on the screen. "That is Baby B. The other is Baby A."

"What?" he and Maren both asked in tandem.

"Twins," he said. "Not identical."

"Twins?" Maren asked. "You're kidding. It can't be twins."

"It is twins. Definitively. That is likely why you feel so drained. And why you are so round."

Maren frowned deeply. "No one likes to be called round," she said.

"It is a shape not a judgment," the doctor said.

"I feel strongly most would disagree with you," Maren grumbled.

"You must eat more," the doctor said. "You have two babies in there. You have to work hard to support them. It is your only job." He looked directly at Acastus. "And your only job is to ensure that she can do hers."

"What can I do?" Acastus said, reeling from this revelation. It felt impossible. It felt unreal.

He had wanted a child to carry on the legacy, and after one very memorable night, they'd made two.

There had been other nights, of course, but there was no doubt in his mind which night had created these twins.

"Feed her. Help her get plenty of rest. There does not seem to be any reason you cannot engage in intercourse." He looked over at Maren who practically bared her teeth at him.

"She does not seem especially high risk. Only fragile for the moment, and there is the usual risk of twins, which is slightly more elevated than that of a single pregnancy. But I will ensure that she is cared for. I will make sure that she gets all the checkups that she needs, and in the in-between, I am trusting you. A man who made a fortune quite so efficiently should have no trouble seeing to the care and keeping of his pregnant wife. She is more important than money, after all."

"Agreed," he said, the words coming out hard through his teeth.

"Then I shall see you again in two weeks. Call me if there is anything unusual."

"Is that it?" Maren asked.

"For now," the doctor said. "And congratulations."

He gathered up his equipment, and vacated, and Maren was still lying in the bed beneath the sheets looking perturbed.

"Twins," she said. "That can't be."

"It is," he said. "You heard yourself."

"But that's not what I… It's not what I imagined," she said.

"It's nowhere near what I imagined either."

"I was trying to imagine one child. But two?"

He decided to keep his own thoughts to himself.

"It will not be terribly different. Will it?"

"I think it will be. It will be twice as much. This child…"

"These children," he said. "I will be here. The truth is, this is not going to be what we imagined. But we must…"

The impossibility of it all, of the things that they believed about their own childhoods, of the thing that he told himself about his mother, and what she told herself about hers, hovered around the edges of his consciousness.

It was a story. Because of course it was. A story that he told himself that his mother was wonderful and the things that she struggled with could not be helped, because he did not know how else to survive it. He had a father who had been apathetic. Weak. And a mother who… Who had demanded too much of him. And when he thought of his own child, that was when he could see it. His own children. He could never be the kind of father his father was, but he could never be a parent in the same fashion his mother was either.

Had he not realized that he needed to be here because he had envisioned his own child having to take care of Maren in a poorly state?

When he shifted the vision of it, onto his own child, when he changed his perception, that was when he saw just how toxic it was.

Just how wrong. And what Maren said echoed within him. Would his children not be enough all on their own? Healthy, and beautiful. His. They would never need to perform for him, they would never need to contort themselves to the puzzle piece that might complete him. It was his job to give them the world, not the other way around.

"You are right, Maren. What my mother did to me was not right," he said. "I was not allowed to have feelings because they could not be supported. Not when hers had to be the most important. I cannot let my father off the hook for what he did. For the way that he relegated her to the back burner of his consciousness. The way that he was content to wait on promises and allow us to be uncomfortable while he pursued them, but you are correct. If my mother had loved him then she would've found contentment in her life. What she wanted was royalty. And she could not attain that, and therefore could not find happiness. Even now she is happy with the title, but does not wish to leave Palermo. She did not come here to thank me. She still blames me, I think. For the long delay of the title. She's not grateful at all, because she always felt as if she deserved it. And for what? She didn't work for it, my father tried. I did, but we were not earning it. We were waiting for a man to give it to us on his whim or not. And then in the end we got it through the means we did. It is yours. I acquired it through marriage, when in contrast at least my riches came from my own work. I lowered myself to take this title. And it still doesn't matter. It still isn't enough."

"I'm sorry to have been so lowering for you," Maren said.

"Not you. The pursuit of it. That I was willing to have it at all costs. Why? Why. It is all tied up in this anger that I feel. Toward him. Toward my father. And never toward my mother. Not ever. But as I tried to imagine parenting these children, I realize that I can no longer shield her from the truth, even in my own heart. She could never be a parent that I would emulate."

Maren stared straight ahead for a moment, and then looked at him. "You're right. You're right to do this. To pull it apart. My father was a psychopath, and it's so easy to blame him for everything. You're right. Our mother left us. Her love couldn't have been that strong if she could leave us. It simply couldn't be.

"She was content to leave us when she had to. To never check back in with us. To never... I'm afraid to get in touch with her. Terrified. Even with my father gone, because what if she rejects me? What if I no longer have the excuse of my father? It just makes me want to remember her from when I was a child. When I can have a simplistic thought on it. Simplistic feelings. It's foolish, I know. But that tells you everything you need to know. I already suspect all of this. But I'm afraid to have it confirmed. I could not… I could not bear it."

"So we no longer believe the story. The fairytale. We must believe the truth. Because it is the only way forward." And they were having twins.

And he felt the same way she did, he could sense it. That they had perhaps had to destroy a cathedral to preserve something greater than a monument. To preserve something sacred. Their children.

They had to be united. They could not be at odds, and they could not be in halfway.

It was far too important an endeavor. Much too much. They could not falter.

"On my life," he said. "Whatever happens between us, I will be there for the children."

"As will I."

The magnitude of all of it settled around them. This could no longer be theoretical. It could no longer be dynastic. It felt far too real now. The stakes far too high. He had made these children along with her, and they owed them a debt. Because when you did not care for your children, he was the end result. The tangled-up wreckage in his chest was the end result.

And Maren was right about one thing, they could not afford to touch one another. For the sake of the children.

This thing was precarious. The peace they might find, the happiness, for the sake of the children. But they had to be careful not to disturb it. Not to introduce anything too volatile, too dangerous.

This was a sacrifice he could bear, to ensure their children had all they needed.

That would be worth it. And maybe it would go a long way in healing him and Maren both.

# CHAPTER TWELVE

MAREN FELT QUEASY as she dialed her sister. Jessie wasn't going to believe this. Maren still couldn't believe it.

"Hello," Jessie said, her voice chipper and bright. And Maren was happy that her sister had occasion to sound that way. She was glad that her sister was happy.

She really was.

"Hi. I have news."

"More news! Good grief," said Jessie.

"I'm having twins."

The silence on the other end was deafening. And satisfying.

"No way," Jessie said.

"I know," she said, covering her face with her hands. "Twins. I can hardly believe it and... He is shocked, you can tell. Like, completely losing his mind, which is fair, because I am too."

"That's... That's big. Good thing the father of your baby is a billionaire, I guess. Your *babies*."

"Yeah," she said, huffing. "Good thing."

But of course he was also an emotionally damaged billionaire, and the problem was, she wasn't entirely certain that she was... Fine.

She went back to the conversation they'd had that morning. About their mothers.

"What do you think of our mother?" she asked Jessie.

"I don't," said Jessie. "She left us."

There was a bit of brittleness in her voice.

"But you're about to be a mother yourself. You must be thinking of her."

"I'm thinking about how I would never do that to my child. No matter what. She could have taken us with her, Maren."

"He would've gone after her."

"I know you're not as far along as I am," said Jessie. "So I know that they aren't like fully formed. I know that you can't feel them move yet. But they're helpless. Growing inside of you. They need you. Now imagine them outside of you, small and vulnerable. You would just leave them? You never ask after them again. Never check in on them. And we know that our mother is out there, that she's fine. She's a socialite, she has a new husband, new children. Half siblings, and she doesn't care."

"I always told myself she had to make herself not care. I always told myself that must be how she was surviving it."

"Maybe that's true," said Jessie. "But it was more important to her to figure out how to survive it than to help us survive. And that's something that I'm having trouble getting over. Truly."

"I really wanted to hold on to her. To my memory of her. But I'm afraid now that I can't afford it. I'm having two babies. I have to… I have to be the best mother that I can. And I think that's going to mean very directly examining what I believe about our childhood. Because I just don't ever want to repeat what our mother and father did."

"I never worried about being Mother. I worried about being our father. Because I'm the one that's a little bit more detached. Or at least I have been." Jessie sighed. "You have always seemed like the conscience, Maren. I always felt like I did good things to make you happy. To try and make myself believe that I wasn't like our father. I felt like you did them because it was easy."

"No, I did them to prove that I was good enough," she whispered. Suddenly her throat went tight. "I did always wonder. How she could leave me. I was her princess. I was so good. I… And all of this. The softness. The way that I dress, the way that I wanted this castle. The way that I am, it was about proving that I was everything she said I was. So that part of it was real. But that was just me. Reaching out and trying to touch a woman who left so long ago that she might not even ever think of me."

"I'm sorry," said Jessie.

"Why did she not love us enough?"

"I don't think either of our parents could."

That echoed inside of Maren for a long time after she got off the phone. Their mother and father hadn't loved them enough. Why?

It made her ache.

She put her hand on her stomach. "I love you both. The most. Enough. It doesn't matter what the relationship is between me and your father, I'm never going to leave you. You will always be mine. I promise. Always."

On shaking legs she walked down to the dining hall, hoping that it would be time for dinner. And when she walked in, her jaw dropped. The long table was covered in a glittering table skate. A Christmas town that glittered and shone with candles and lights, gold reindeer all around. There were Christmas trees set at different heights on the table, gold and green and red. And all around the room were real trees, lit up with white lights.

"Oh, my," she said.

It felt like magic. It felt like the sort of fairytale she was trying to tell herself she didn't need. But, oh, how she felt like she might need it.

"I hope this is to your liking."

She looked up, and saw him standing in the doorway, dressed spectacularly for dinner in a dark blue suit. He was so beautiful it made her hurt.

He was the fairytale. Standing there in the middle of it, gloriously handsome and surrounded by all of this holiday sparkle.

But she couldn't afford to indulge.

She had to be practical. Because she couldn't turn away from the truth.

He didn't love her. And they were tangled-up messes of people. Who needed to find a way to be good parents for their children.

And this was just him following the doctor's orders.

With Christmas decorations. It was the season, after all.

"This is beautiful," she said.

"The staff did it, of course, not me."

"I know," she said, holding back a laugh at the image of him up on a little ladder putting a star on top of the tree.

Except then suddenly it didn't seem so funny. Except then suddenly it made her ache just slightly.

What kind of father would he be? Would he want to do domestic things? Silly things?

Their twins weren't identical. They could have one of each. A boy and a girl. How would he be with the daughter? Would he be soft? And with the son, would he be too rigid? Or would he model strength in an interesting way? Would he teach his son that he could have feelings as well? How could he do that when he didn't have any of his own?

"What?"

"Just thinking about the fact that we're having two children," she said. "It's unavoidable. I am... Overwhelmed by it."

"You have no need to be overwhelmed. We will of course get nannies."

But she knew that nannies wouldn't solve the issue of their needing to be parents. They might be able to have this, but they would have to work for it.

They were both wounded adults, who wanted badly not to wound their children in the same fashion.

They didn't have time to move straight into that discussion, though, because the meal was brought out. A spectacular array of roasted meat and vegetables, orzo and pitas.

She was so hungry, she thought that she could eat all of it without help.

It was amazing how her appetite had turned around... Since he'd arrived.

She pushed that thought to the side.

She piled food onto her plate, and he did the same.

She took a bite of a dolma, and chewed slowly. "The thing is," she said. "It's so much easier to see the issues in our childhood when I began to think of them being done to... Well, a child. One that isn't me. I had Jessie, and we survived, so it was easy for me to think that what was asked of us wasn't too much. But of course it was. Of course it was. We were children being asked to work with a violent criminal. Children who were left to live with a violent criminal. And while I will always carry some sympathy in my heart for my mother, the truth is, she loved herself the most."

"Yes," said Acastus, looking down at his plate. "The truth is, I have spent my life protecting my mother because no one else did. It is hard for me to condemn her in any fashion."

"But who protected you?" she asked.

"I would've told you that I didn't need it. I always felt like a man. More of one than my father. I was always so angry about what he wasn't doing, that I felt I always did. I always felt as if it was my calling, my responsibility. But when I think back on the time spent here. The time in the dungeon."

"How long were you there?"

"Two months, I think."

She gasped. She thought he was thrown down there for a couple of hours as a performative gesture. It never occurred to her that he had been kept there. Like a real prisoner.

"Over jewels that they recovered?"

"Yes," he said. "But this is it. My mother was so upset. Weeping and wailing over what we lost. She never acted as if she cared about my time spent in the dungeon. I accepted that at the time because it seemed… I was willing to take everything on board.

I was willing to let it be all my fault. Anything to counteract the way my father made her feel."

"You were a child. Stealing jewelry for his mother, and the fact that she made you feel as if she needed that to be happy and not your safety, that you needed to do things for her and not… Simply be her son, that says everything."

"I do not like to think of it. I do not like to accept it. It is only because we are having children of our own that I am even…"

"Because you know it would be wrong," she said. "You know it would be wrong to do that to them."

"I think of the ways in which my parents live their life. The way my father was a husband, who lived as though nothing had changed. He acted as if he had no wife and child. My mother acted as if her husband and child existed to serve her. And that is why I recognize that we cannot just expect to do this right. We cannot."

"I agree," she said. She looked around the palace. It was so isolated. It sat on a rock. It was beautiful. And she loved it. But she realized something.

"We cannot raise children here," she said.

There was a strange sort of glint in his eyes.

"Why not?"

"Think about your childhood. I'll think about mine. We were so isolated. We were cut off."

"Yes. But…"

"A title isn't going to make our child happy. They

need to have friends. More than just each other. They need to have something normal. You and I both know what it's like to not have normal."

"Spending time in a dungeon is a little bit beyond that."

"I know. But I don't think… I don't think we can make a life here."

"But the title…"

"It's ceremonial. We'll still have it. We can spend time here. But our children need to be able to go to school. They need to be able to be around friends. To go to their houses."

"We will discuss that later."

She could feel his resistance to it, and she did understand. Of course, his life was defined by the pursuit of this place. She could understand why it felt too painful for him to let go of it.

And suddenly it all felt a bit impossible. This endeavor.

Their marriage.

How could they make a life together and never touch? How could they make a family?

"Of course… We don't have to live together," she said.

He looked up. "We don't?"

"Why? We aren't a couple? It would be entirely possible for our children to come here every weekend and be with you. You can have whatever you want, and I can give them normal during the week. We can coparent."

There was something thunderous on his face. *"Coparent?"*

"Yes. It's… It's a very modern thing to do, really. There's nothing wrong with it."

"No," he said.

"No?"

"No," he said again, definitively.

"But that's insane. We're trying to make something functional and…"

"And we will not do it by breaking apart the household."

"What good did it do your parents to stay together? What good did it ever do you? I think you know that nothing good came of it. Your mother stayed with your father, and for what reason? So that she could use him continually to manipulate you?"

"Enough," he said. "Don't forget—"

"What? The foundation of this is that I was manipulated into this marriage, into this conception?"

"I believe," he said, "the word you're looking for is *seduced.*"

And it was as if all the civility from the last few hours evaporated. She remembered. The passion. The intensity between them. Everything.

She remembered it, and she craved it.

Suddenly, it seemed like a joke that only moments ago they had been trying to construct a mature and careful plan for how to raise their children. That they had been attempting to pull apart their past pain. Because suddenly it all felt so close to the surface. Suddenly they had hit a disagreement, and it was like they had been lit on fire.

They were not friends, that was the problem.

There were moments where she felt like she liked him, but the truth remained, he was the man who had forced her into a marriage. She ignored the voice inside of her that reminded her she had a way out. Several. That she had caved completely when presented with choices she didn't like, and that she had been happily under his spell when she had allowed him to seduce her. That she had pushed him for sex the first time, and had pursued him for it after that as well.

That she was the one who lay around full of malaise when he was gone.

Yes, she conveniently forgot all of that. She focused on what an autocrat he was. On how he had done something no sane person would ever do.

She focused on all of that. Because it made her feel good. Because it made her anger feel justified.

"We're going to do what's best for our children. It isn't going to be about your legacy."

"I told you from the beginning…"

"Yes. And everything changed today. You know that it did. You know it changed."

"Enough," he thundered. "Perhaps you're right. Perhaps something does need to change. We tried.

We tried to do it your way. We tried to do it my way. I left. And you dissolved."

"Don't give yourself all that much credit. I was ill. And pregnant. It was hardly my fault."

"Whatever the reason," he said. "You were reduced. I cannot stay away. And we…"

He shook his head. "This cannot be ignored."

He pushed his chair back, and came around to her side of the table. "I think the real problem lies between us. You speak of coparenting as if this is deniable. As if when we are part we're not miserable."

"Look at us now," she said. "Are we less miserable when we're together?"

"I burn for you," he said. "It is not happiness, but when I am away it is unendurable. And I cannot… I cannot be here, I cannot stand here next to you and not have you."

She shook her head, her heart thundering wildly. "No. It was never what it was about, it was…"

"I know," he said. "But it doesn't matter. We never set out to have twins either. And when we were together it was never all about conception, and you know it well."

"But we're dysfunctional."

"Yes. And we are dysfunctional even when we are not lovers. We will live together. And you will be mine," he said. "You will be in my bed every night. I will have you until we are both mindless with our passion."

"What about the children?"

"They will be there. Of course. As you said, this is for them. But why engage in this farce? Why act like it was not our passion that created them? It was. It is a miraculous thing. We were never lying there thinking of England."

"But if we burn each other to the ground, our children will be caught in the flames."

"You were just here. There should not have been flames, and there were. You are acting as if we can go to a moment where we have no feelings for one another, and I believe you and I both know that isn't true. That isn't reasonable. They're already there. There is no protecting us or the children from what already exists. So let us burn then."

And with that, he lifted her from the chair, and claimed her mouth with his own.

He knew that it was counter to anything logical. To anything reasonable. He did know that.

He knew that he was accomplishing nothing through this proclamation. He knew that it was wrong. That he was putting them both in a more precarious position than should be allowed.

But he could think of nothing but the need roaring through his veins. Could think of nothing but the insult of the two of them living separately.

It had become clear to him the moment that he had first touched her that there would be no other lovers for him. And that he would not be able to abide there being any other lovers for her.

It was clear.

It was clear that whatever their intent they were not what they had hoped.

He didn't know how this fit into anything. Into the swirling mass of emotion that tangled in his chest like a bramble and threatened to destroy him. He didn't know why he was doing this. Except there was no other choice. Coparenting. This idea of living separate. This idea of…

Of being a man who cannot keep his family together. That was what it was. He could not allow it. He would give his child everything because what other option was there? He would give his child everything because his parents had been lost in all of these unfulfilled promises. He would make a promise now. To her. To the children.

By God, he would be a man who made things right.

So he kissed her. And he ignored the truth. That there was a monster inside of him who needed this for reasons that had nothing to do with their children. That there was something in him crying out for fulfillment.

This made sense now, and he needed it to. Wanted it to. Was desperate for it to.

This was everything he had ever needed. Ever wanted. This was something…

That made him feel so far away from the helpless boy he'd been in this place.

And he kissed her. Kissed her because he wanted to. Because he needed to. Because perhaps all along she had been the promise to be fulfilled. Because perhaps from the very beginning this had been what he needed.

Perhaps from the very beginning it had been her.

Maybe this was destiny.

Perhaps he owed his father thank you.

And that nearly made him want to laugh, but instead he growled into her mouth, and allowed himself the satisfaction of swallowing her cry of pleasure that climbed up her throat.

"Tell me you want me," he growled.

She looked at him, a wildness in her eyes. He took a step back. "Tell me," he said.

If she no longer wanted him, he did not know what he would do. He was Acastus. Never, ever, had a woman not wanted him. And if Maren did not want him, then nothing else mattered. None of the previous women, none of his previous achievements. Nothing mattered at all. If he had succeeded in taking her desire for him and extinguishing it with his actions, then...

He felt something helpless scrabble in his chest, and it reminded him of being in a dungeon. Of being at the mercy of somebody else. He was. Now. He was that child with a mother who threw things, who wailed and cried and needed him to be strong. He was that child. Who had done something in an effort to appease the person that he loved most, and found himself imprisoned.

He was helpless. Storm-tossed and wrecked.

And then she said, a whisper, barely audible, "I want you."

And triumph roared through him. A need fulfilled like he had never before known.

He wrapped his arms around her, holding her firmly to his chest. "Mine," he growled.

They were no longer talking about the future of their children.

This no longer had anything to do with custody arrangements or anything he had told himself before.

This was about him. Her.

This was about this great, aching need within him that he could not see the end of.

This was about a deficit in the very depths of his soul that he could not grasp hold of. That he could not explain, but with all the money that he had attained in the years since he had left this place, he could not erase.

So he kissed her, because there was nothing else.

And he carried her out of the room, into the fireside room, and set her down on a blanket beneath the Christmas tree.

"Tell me," he said roughly.

"Acastus," she said, putting her fingertips on his cheek. "I want you."

"You do not wish to live separate from me," he said.

She shook her head.

"You wish to live with me," he growled. "You want me."

"I want you," she said.

He could not stop the words that were pouring out of his mouth. He could not stop the need. The hunger, that rolled inside of him like a dragon.

He couldn't.

There was nothing that he could do to staunch the desperate flow.

He stripped his shirt off, everything else, and looked down at her. She was a present. One that he would unwrap slowly.

He began to undo the intricate knots around her dress. Loosened the silken material and exposed the pale curves of her body to his eyes.

She was wearing a red lace bra, and matching underwear, that fired an inferno in his gut.

The roundness of her stomach was a glory. And he touched her with all the reverence he had felt that the doctor had not given her.

He moved his hand slowly over her curves, watched the contrast between them. The rough masculinity of his hands over that soft femininity.

It was a glorious contrast. It made him feel strong and weak all at once.

And he would've said that he could not glory in any sort of weakness. And yet before her, he did.

She arched her back, and he answered her, pulling the lace cups of the bra down and exposing her breasts to his gaze.

He bent down and claimed one pale, tightened bud with his tongue, sucked her deep into his mouth.

He teased her there until she cried out. Until everything was his.

Until she was his.

He stripped her bare, gloried in the feel of her, the taste. Pushed her further, harder, higher than ever before.

He brought her to the edge repeatedly. Until she was sobbing his name. Until she was a mess of tears and pleas and somehow it still wasn't enough to appease that beast within him that had woken up. That had decided it wanted everything. Needed everything. All that she was.

All that she would ever be.

When he finally thrust inside of her, she shattered. Calling out his name. And she pulled from him a climax that nearly decimated him. That shattered a piece of his soul he hadn't known still existed.

They lay there like that, beneath the tree. And he had never thought much about Christmas, or the miracles that people professed to find that time of year. Had never known magic, spiritual or pagan, beneath the Christmas tree, and in that moment he felt both. In a way that he could not explain.

At that moment, he felt her, in a way he would never be able to understand or articulate.

But he knew there would be no more discussion of them living apart. Of them not touching one another, because it would be impossible. Because it was untenable.

Because they were this. Whatever else there was in the world, they were this.

He had not set out to find this. It had never been an idea in his head.

But when he had seen her for the first time, he had known that she was beautiful. In ways that he had not anticipated. In ways he could have never guessed. And it was only more true now. Beauty had not even been a scratch at the surface.

He had looked at her, and he had known she was his. It was a gift he had not anticipated, and yet it was one he would not question. It was one he would take. Without reservation.

She looked up at him, her expression soft, something deep in her eyes that he wanted. That he wanted to claim. That he wanted for his own.

"You will move into my room," he said.

"I like my room," she said.

"Then I will move into yours," he said, because suddenly compromise did not seem so difficult.

"Okay," she said softly. "That would be acceptable."

"There will be no more discussions of us being apart," he said.

He picked her up then, and she grinned.

"What?"

"I like it when you carry me."

"Well, then I will make sure to do it more often."

She snuggled against him, and he struggled to fully comprehend the whiplash of the last hour. Calm rational discussion, burning over into a fight, which had then become… This.

And his heart felt like it might be two sizes larger than it had been when this had all begun.

He wasn't sure if he liked it. But he couldn't deny it either.

She was a singular woman. This woman who had been raised by a criminal, and remembered every single thing.

Who had been abandoned by her mother, and who had tried her very best to love that woman anyway.

He could understand needing to care for a flawed parent.

She was such a strange and singular creature and somehow, she was the one person he had ever met who recognized something within him. That made that thing in him raise its head and look. For connection. For something more.

He had come into this cold. Acting out of a sense of duty.

And then they had tried to pull everything apart and rationalize it.

Now he felt like they were in a fast-moving vehicle careening toward something. Whether that be a cliff or safety, he didn't know.

And it filled him with a sense of disquiet to realize that connection to another person could create this level of uncertainty. For he was a man of control. A man who had done his level best to always feel certain in his life.

And this thing with her undid that.

And yet he could not go back. That measured conversation they'd been having had been false.

But he did not know what this meant for their future. The future of their children.

It was quite impossible to say.

He laid her down in her bed, and he lay beside her.

He had not truly allowed himself to sleep with her the nights when they'd made love before. Instead, he had dozed just barely, then turned over to take her when the need arose within him again.

And this time, he just pulled her against him, swathed them both in blankets and allowed himself to sleep.

Because later he would find out what they were careening toward. Later there would be consequences for this recklessness. Maybe.

But for the first time in his life, he was putting them on hold.

He was releasing his control.

And giving it to her.

# CHAPTER THIRTEEN

SHE LAY THERE, awake in the wee hours, feeling the best that she had for a very long time.

Acastus was there with his arms wrapped around her.

Maybe that was it. Maybe that was why.

Suddenly, an aching cavern opened up inside of her chest.

This was not how it was supposed to be. It wasn't supposed to be about them. She had tried so hard to... To minimize her feelings for him. She had tried to be rational, after all, what was the point of having a brain like hers if she couldn't be logical with it. Rational. Reasonable.

But she was a dreamer. She always had been. She was the one with the mind palace. The one who longed to be a princess. She wished she could be different. She wished her fantasies hadn't rushed away from her.

She had wanted to be logical for her child. Because she had wanted to avoid...

She just didn't want to be hurt. That was the bottom line. It wasn't really about avoiding being like her parents. He was nothing like her father. She wasn't her mother, she knew that too. She wouldn't leave. But she had been left. Abandoned. Hurt. And it was what scared her now.

It was just she knew what it was like to simply not be enough. To not be enough to keep a person with her. To not be enough at all. Ever.

And the idea of being that for Acastus, it terrified her.

She wanted to be logical. She wasn't.

She was in this moment a creature of absolute need. Of feeling. That she had no control over. That she couldn't rationalize or con her way out of.

She turned over and looked at him. He was beautiful when he slept. But not softer.

The man was carved from granite.

He had been thrown in a dungeon here. His mother had depended on him to be strong, and he had fashioned himself into something impossibly mighty, but how did a person reach a man who'd had to build himself up that way?

She had always been far too easy to reach. Her life should have made it harder. She had never managed it.

And right now, she ached with her own softness.

A tear slid down her cheek and she dashed it away. Even as she sat there, taking in the way that he looked in sleep. Because she would have this image with her for the rest of her life, and she would call upon it whenever she missed him.

The idea of missing him made her want to howl in pain. She also knew that she couldn't discount that it might happen.

She knew that.

"You're staring," he said without opening his eyes.

"Well," she said. "You're very handsome."

"Thank you." She heard a smile in his voice, even though his lips did not form one.

"Acastus," she said. "Tell me about being in the dungeon."

"Why?" He did open his eyes then.

"Because I'm trying to imagine it. You here and… Captive."

"It's exactly as you would think. This was its own sovereign nation, and Stavros Argos was the master of it. He put me in shackles, had his security guards lead me down there. He kept me chained. He was afraid of me, as he should have been. I was seventeen and could have easily overtaken him even then."

She felt as if she'd been stabbed. "You were a child," she said.

He shook his head. "I was a man. I had to be one. Because my father…"

"You're very angry at your father."

"She was his responsibility," he said. "It actually does not matter if she was difficult. My father married her, I did not. But I couldn't let her sink into despair. I had to take care of her. Because he wouldn't. He was about what he felt Stavros owed him and nothing more. He could not see past the fact that it wouldn't matter in the end if the promises had been fulfilled because of all the damage he had done. All of the damage… It was so much. I understand that. I was in chains long before I was in chains here. I had to take on the responsibility of being the man of our family because my father would not."

Her chest ached for him. She didn't know what it was like to have to take responsibility. That hadn't been her life. That hadn't been the particular trauma that she and her sister had endured.

They had simply been manipulated into being their father's things.

"I wanted to be good," she said. "And from the time I was a child I was aware that I was… A villain. It was really difficult. To want to be something else. And I did. I wanted it so much. So badly. But I couldn't choose it. My father was in charge of us. Of what we could do. Of how we used our minds."

"And if you could choose," he said. "If you could choose what to do with your mind, what would you choose?"

She felt hollowed out and sad in that moment. Because she wasn't sure how to answer the question. She wasn't sure of so many things.

"I knew that I wanted to be safe. I knew that I wanted to not be alone. I won this castle, and I wanted to be a princess. But none of that's doing anything, is it?"

"You don't have to do anything," he said. "If these are your dreams, then they're fine dreams."

"Sure I want to be a good mother," she said. "I know that. Beyond that, I'm not really sure. I do wonder sometimes what I might've been if I hadn't started life in that compound. Though the reality is, a brain like mine is most useful to a criminal. Someone who is trying not to leave paper trails. I can store everything in my head instead of in files. Practically speaking, in the rest of the world, it's more of a party trick than it is anything necessary. So I don't know. I'm probably deluding myself thinking that I could have contributed something if I had a traditional education. A different life. The truth is, I like to believe that I would've been good. But what does that even mean? Look at what I've done with my life since we've escaped. I engaged in cons to better myself. My station. And even though I can justify it all, because of the kind of men who were making those bets, even though I can tell myself I was being like Robin Hood, and not just a regular con artist, I don't have a lot of evidence that I'm actually good. Left to my own devices, who knows."

"You are good, Maren. I think that's apparent. I don't think you need to worry. In fact, I think a truly bad person doesn't worry at all whether or not they are good."

"I suppose. I guess the real question is I don't know if I'm good or just sad. I don't know if I'm especially aching to be a good mother, or if I just want these children to love me. I just…" Her own longing took her breath away. "It's so difficult. Really. I loved my mother so very much. And she left me. She walked away from me when I needed her. It has always been hard for me to believe that there weren't just some things about me that made me easy to leave."

"You were not easy for me to leave."

His words came close to healing something inside of her. Begin to mend a crack in her soul that she hadn't realized was there. She couldn't respond. All the words just got bottled up in her throat. And she let them sit there. She let herself rest.

Because right now they were together. Right now she didn't need to know what she wanted to do for evermore. Or if she was good, or if she would even be a good mother. Right now, she knew that she was being held by Acastus. And right now, that was all that mattered. Just this moment. Just their breathing. Just the Christmas decorations outside, and the passion between them. The rest… The rest would be for later.

But this was now. And it was good.

And there had been spare few moments in her life for which that could be said.

So she just decided to rest. No con, no catch, no waiting for the other shoe to drop. It was the best sleep she could ever remember having. And maybe, just maybe, they could make a family. Maybe she could begin to have dreams.

Maybe they could begin to make something new.

She would cling to that hope. And cling to it hard.

# CHAPTER FOURTEEN

As CHRISTMAS DREW nearer Maren began to feel lighter. Perhaps it had nothing to do with the holiday, but maybe it did. She was so happy with him. So happy with this life that they were building for themselves.

And some of her fears about whether or not they would be like her parents had abated. They did fight sometimes. Because Maren was dramatic. And she owned that. She enjoyed a good fight, it turned out. She liked to be seen and heard. And one thing that was apparent, one thing that mattered quite a bit was that Acastus was a safe place for her to vent that anger. He was safe. In general. And that was a gift, she knew.

Her life felt full. The impending birth of their children feeling like a gift. She had Jessie now, and Ewan. Their baby. She had Acastus, and she had the promise of impending motherhood.

Jessie and Ewan came for a pre-Christmas dinner and Jessie was thrilled to see her niece and her sister.

She held her, on her hip, and snuggled her soft baby head.

"She only gets more beautiful, Jessie," said Maren.

"She looks a little bit like her aunt," said Jessie, stroking the baby's downy red hair.

"I guess she does."

"I can't believe that you're going to have twins," said Jessie, putting her hands on Maren's stomach, the only person who would ever be allowed to do that, other than Acastus of course.

She looked up at her husband. "Neither could we."

"That doesn't run in your family, does it?" Ewan asked.

"Who cares if it does," said Jessie happily. "You are absolutely loaded, and we can afford it."

"I'm not sure that my nerves could take it," he said.

Jessie waved a hand. "Your nerves are fine, Ewan. And you and I both know it. We're both gamblers."

"That is true," Ewan said.

Then Acastus asked about their gambling, and off the two of them went to the races, talking about their triumphs and losses in casinos.

Both of them had been playing a game, Ewan working to disgrace his title and the name of his father in order to get revenge, Jessie to make a life for them apart from their father.

It was amazing the way that their own issues were parallel, much the way that hers and Acastus's were.

They were both circling this idea of love and passion, and yet they had found passion, it couldn't be denied. And in all of these little ways she was seeing how it was different. Even this, welcoming her sister and her sister's husband, spending time together, it proved that they weren't the same as their parents.

It really did.

She had lived in a home, too. A rather large one. But it hadn't been this.

This place that was decked out in Christmas decor, and filled with warmth.

This place that was utterly and completely safe. This place that promised her healing and family.

She had never experienced anything like it before.

She wondered if he had.

He had been held in the dungeon here. He had been treated like a servant. And yet it was different now. They had staff for the palace, but they treated no one like they were beneath them. It simply wasn't in either of their characters.

And that, she was beginning to understand, mattered.

It wasn't passion itself that was bad, but the people the passion was between.

That was the potential issue. That was the thing that you had to worry about.

She had married a good man. Through no merit

of her own really. She had shown up, and they were married. And over the months, even though there had been time with little contact between them, she felt that when he needed to prove that he was good, he did.

She had spent a lot of time worrying about being good. She had spent a lot of time worrying about a great many things. She didn't worry about that anymore. She felt good. She felt happy. And she accepted that as the truth of the matter more than anything else.

Because hadn't she and Jessie endured enough? Endured enough wickedness and pain to know something good when they saw it? She might've questioned it before. But not now. She hadn't planned this. And she had planned so many things in her life. Masterminded so many things. But not this. Never this.

She hadn't been able to manipulate it, con it, none of it. They had met purely because she had won that poker game. It was chance and fate all rolled into one, but it was them that had made it something real.

The electricity between them. It was not something that could've been planned. Never in a thousand years. She knew that. And it was what made this feel like perhaps it was something she could trust. Just maybe. Just maybe.

She wanted to talk to him about it. She wanted to tell him. She proposed to wait until Christmas, because it was… It was her gift to him.

A laying bare of her soul.

It was the day before Christmas Eve. She and her sister had both agreed that they would have actual Christmas at their own homes. A chance to establish tradition for the first time.

They both understood each other, and the need to do that, because they understood where they had come from.

Before she and Ewan left on Christmas Eve morning, Jessie leaned in and gave Maren a kiss on the cheek. "He's gorgeous," she said.

Maren shimmered inside. "I know," she said. "He really is."

"Be happy with him," said Jessie.

"I want to be," she said.

"What's keeping you from total happiness?"

"I'm afraid. I'm afraid because I think I'm falling in love with him, and I want to tell him, but I'm afraid that it's going to make him… I'm afraid that he'll run away from me."

Maren looked at her, considering. "He might. But that doesn't mean that you won't be able to get him back. Ewan had such a difficult childhood, and you know that he turned away from what we had. More than once. Because it was difficult, to accept that no matter how much he had wanted to run away from emotion. From love, it had found him anyway."

"But I don't know how to get away from the fear… Because our mother didn't love us enough, Jessie.

And I can't bear the idea that he might not love me enough. To get over his pain."

"You can't think of it that way," said Jessie. "I get that it might feel that way. But the truth is, that wound that you carry inside of you, all these things that we remember with perfect clarity, people feel all those things just the same, even if they can't recall the situation in as perfect detail as we can. It doesn't mean that the pain of whatever he's gone through has faded. It lives in his soul. An imprint and a memory. You can't be afraid that he doesn't love you enough, because even if he rejects you, that isn't really what's happening. Even with our mother, I don't believe that's what was happening."

"You don't?"

"I think people run from pain. If the house is on fire, you're going to try to escape, and maybe later you'll regret the things and people you left behind, but all you can think about is the way the flames are burning you. I think that's what our mother was dealing with. She was leaving a burning house. She left us to burn. That's the truth. But she could only think of her own pain. It was the pain that was bigger. Not the love that was too small."

"So what's the solution? I ignore the pain? I ignore the fear?"

"I actually think that's all you can do. And in a year, I trust that I'm going to be standing here with you, your beautiful children, and your husband who loves you very much. But you're going to have to take the risk."

Maren felt desolate. "Why can't he take the risk?"

"He could. You could wait. You could wait so that you're not pushing him off of the cliffs into a pool of your feelings. But do you really have the patience, Maren? I don't think that's you. You're the one that went and got Ewan for me. You're the one that couldn't stand to see me upset. You pushed both of us before we were ready. If you don't do the same to Acastus, that just makes you a hypocrite, doesn't it?"

"You're very annoying," said Maren.

"I know. But it's out of love. The same that you have for me."

"Maybe I'll just keep it to myself."

"You could. There is nothing that says you have to be the brave one."

But she knew that she would be. She knew that she had to be. She didn't know why, only that she did. She and Jessie had been unloved long enough, that was the thing. She wanted what Jessie had. And she wanted… Most of all she wanted her happiest memories to not be ones that lived in her mind palace. She had this palace. They were having children. It was Christmas. She wanted her happiest life to be in front of her. Not just reliant on those images that she carried with her.

She couldn't fix that thing with her mother. But perhaps she could make something new.

She could have that love, that imperfect love from the past, and she could have love now.

Maybe Jessie was right. Maybe that was worth a fight.

"I'll let you know how it goes," Maren said.

"I have no doubt you will."

She waved them off as they got into a plush boat that would take them back to the mainland.

Jessie didn't like the idea of flying in a helicopter with the baby, and Maren really couldn't blame her. She would be defaulting to a boat from now on too.

It was funny how everything felt precarious and precious now. She and Jessie had spent their lives risk-taking. Gambling. So much of it not being of their own choice, but then later some of it being of their own making. And this would be the ultimate gamble. The ultimate gamble on a secure and lovely life. On the things she wanted most.

If Acastus were to ask her now what she wanted, being a princess or having his heart, she knew the answer.

That morning, she had toast and orange juice put out at the table. And when he came in, she looked up at him. "Have a seat," she said.

He arched a brow. "Are you asking me to have toast and orange juice with you?"

"I believe our goalposts have changed, don't you?"

"I suppose they have," he acknowledged, sitting down across from her. "Not really a holiday spread."

"Well, dinner last night with my sister was a very rich affair, and unfortunately, even though I need to eat all day, I can't eat very much at once these days."

"Poor Maren," he said.

But then he did sit down, and he did pick up his toast.

And her whole heart went tight.

Because maybe this was it. Maybe it was something. Maybe this was a sign.

A sign that he had changed his mind about what their marriage would entail. Well, she knew he had. She didn't say anything, not then, because she had a plan.

"I wish for you to open a present tonight," she said.

"Okay."

"I would like to have dinner in my study, as you call it. By the fire. By the Christmas tree."

"If it suits you," he said.

She spent the day jangling with nerves, and when she came down to meet him for dinner, her heart nearly stopped. Because he was stunningly beautiful in his tuxedo, his olive skin a glorious contrast to the crisp white shirt, his dark hair pushed back off his forehead. No one would ever know that he had been a servant in this place. He looked every inch the immaculate billionaire. And yet he had been. He carried the scars and the pain. He had done all this for his mother and she wasn't here.

Maren knew that pain.

She understood it. She understood him.

She loved him. It was that simple.

And she was willing to risk for it.

For her part, she was dressed only in a short silk robe.

She delighted in that. The mismatch in their attire. She often liked to be naked while he was fully dressed. Liked the feeling of being pressed against the fine fabrics that he wore. Of the power that he had in those moments.

And in turn, the power that she had. To drive him wild.

"I have overdressed," he said.

"You're perfect," she said.

Dinner had already been served, and she sat down with him on the floor by the Christmas tree and served him. Watched as he ate fruit and cheese.

"I thought tonight that it would be my turn to draw a bath for you."

She already had some of the household staff seeing to that.

"For me?"

"Yes. I rather enjoyed the experience of you taking care of me. I thought you should have it in kind."

His eyes were alight with erotic interest.

She loved the way he made her feel. About her

changing body. She was never insecure when it came to him, because he made it so clear how deeply attractive he found her.

She led him to the large bathroom, and began to slowly strip his clothes from him. She undid his black tie, his shirt, pushed his jacket from his shoulders.

She knelt down and untied his shoes, removed his socks.

She devoted herself wholly to the erotic art of undressing him. Of unveiling every strong, sinewy line of his body. That golden skin, the rough hair on his chest and stomach.

She kissed him there. Then down further. She curved her hand around his stunning arousal and took him into her mouth, unable to wait.

He gripped her hair, guiding her movements as she swallowed him down.

"This is not a bath," he said, his voice rough as his hips flexed, driving him to the back of her throat.

"Is that a complaint?" she asked, moving away from him to ask the question.

"Never," he said, and she swallowed him again.

Then she stood, satisfied that she had teased him enough, removing her robe, and exposing her curves to his gaze. "Now get in, regrettably I can't pick you up."

He smiled, and slid beneath the water. She nearly groaned as the ripples covered up her view of his body.

But she was equally satisfied when she began to move the water over his hard muscles, making him slick.

She worked his hardness beneath the surface of the water, her hand moving up and down over his impressive length.

And then she abandoned the intimate touch, and moved to his shoulders, stroking him, rubbing him. Easing the tension in his muscles.

She moved her hands down his chest, up beneath his jaw. She kissed him. She showed him how much she cared with every stroke of her hands over his body.

He had always taken such care with her. With her pleasure.

She wanted to do the same for him.

"Join me," he said roughly.

He pulled her into the bath, and she positioned herself over his hardness, sinking down onto him and taking him in deep.

Her breath hissed through her teeth as they began to move, cushioned by the water, the buoyancy helping make her feel lighter. More able to move.

He gripped her rear and brought her down hard onto him, establishing a hard rhythm that challenged them both.

And when they came, it was together. Gasping and panting.

And what happened next just seemed right. Seemed obvious.

What happened next was nothing less than her speaking the truth. "I love you."

She could feel him go stiff. Could feel his denial.

"Let's get dressed," he said, his voice hard.

They did, and went into the bedroom. The one that they shared.

"Perhaps I will stay in my room tonight," he said.

The words sent a trickle of dread through her. He was separating himself from her. Because she had not given him a burden to carry, she'd given him her love. And he had no idea what to do with it. Or perhaps he didn't know how to see love as anything but a boulder, and he had to shun it.

He was doing it. Pulling away. Exactly as Jessie had said that he might. And it had always been incumbent upon Maren to decide if it was worth the risk.

Was he worth it?

Was the ultimate happiness they might find worth it?

*Yes.*

A painful, twisted answer bloomed in her soul. It wasn't a simple or easy answer. But it was honest.

She had wanted to be a princess. But that had been a simplistic metaphor for wanting happiness. Protection.

She couldn't have that without him, she realized now. But not half of him. All of him. All that they could be, and if she allowed him distance, if she pushed down her feelings and denied them, she would be a princess with a castle, yes.

But she would not live happily ever after.

He was the one thing she had to have.

All of this could slide into the sea. It was him she wanted.

His love.

"If your intent on pulling away from me, don't do it by inches," she said. "If that makes you want to leave, then I would prefer that you leave. At least that would be honest."

"You're my wife," he said. "I will not leave you, nor the children."

"You will just condemn me to a life of your ambivalence?"

"I'm not ambivalent. What about any of this gives you the sense that I don't care?"

"It feels…"

"Enough. It is not about what it feels like. I… Love is a prison, Maren. And it is not one that I will step into."

"I didn't think you were worried about yourself."

"Well, I am," he said. "I was imprisoned here. For love. How can I forget?"

"And it earned you nothing. But I'm not asking you to go to prison for me. I want you to open yourself up. I want you to be my husband. Really. We signed the paper. We didn't speak about vows. We didn't pledge undying love. But I want to do it now. I promise myself to you, Acastus. I promise to love you, to honor you, to obey you as you do me. I promise to give you all of myself. For better or worse. Even if somehow we fall into poverty. I would never price being a princess over being your wife. I would be your wife even if we were here scrubbing floors."

"No," he said. "I just… I can't…"

"Why? What are you afraid of?"

He looked at her, and she could see the fear in his eyes. Real fear. She would never doubt it or question it. She knew it to be honest. He was not trying to hurt her. He really was trapped in a burning house. She knew that it was real.

"I am your wife," she said. "And you are my husband. We are having children. If you leave, then what? If you leave like my mother, to escape this, the big feelings. Then what?"

"I'm not leaving," he said.

But she could see that he wanted to. "Stay with me. Your mother used you. She manipulated you. Your feelings. You didn't get a chance to have them. Tell me. Tell me everything. Everything you fear. Everything you desire. Tell me. It matters to me."

He sat down on the edge of the bed. "I… I am angry. My father did nothing to protect me. To protect me from his wife's emotions, and my mother did nothing to thank me for all that I did. Everyone around her was at fault. Including me. It didn't matter how hard I tried. It didn't matter what I did. I couldn't ever be enough. Even now, this isn't enough. I married you for her sake. Conceived children because it was what she wanted me to do. I earned billions, to keep her in a lifestyle to which she wanted to become accustomed, and it was clear that what she actually wanted was the lifestyle. Not me, never me. I… I was never enough."

"But you are," she said. "You are. We are together. We are married. If we separate, what end does it serve? If we turn away from this, then we are our parents. I refuse to be. I refuse. I love you. I want that more than I want to be safe. I want you more than I want things to be easy. I have chosen to fight for this even though I knew that you might not be able to say that you loved me yet. But I want you to know it's what I want."

"We never had a chance," he said, his voice rough. "What if I'm unable to give you all the things you dream of? What if I can't give you what you need, then shouldn't I set you free to be with someone who can?"

"I don't want someone else. You are the father of my children. And that is a cop-out."

They talked. Endlessly. Until their voices were hoarse. About pain and loss. About the ways in which their parents had failed them.

"It's Christmas morning," she said, croaking out the words.

"Come with me," he said.

She took his hand. They were both naked, but the palace was asleep, and they slipped down to a part of the palace she'd never been before.

The dungeon.

He didn't dress to go to the dungeon. It was symbolic of everything that he'd been through here. The humiliation. The pain. But he needed her to understand. He was exhausted from fighting with her. From fighting himself.

He needed her to see. He needed her to understand.

The weight of it.

The great, inglorious burden.

"This was the biggest gesture I could give to my mother. It was not yet enough. I wanted so badly to be enough for her, and I could not be. And I... This has been the prison I remained in. You're correct. Because I thought by staying in it I could somehow keep myself from ever being locked up against my will again. I don't want to be in here anymore. I want you. I want whatever life we can have. Whatever life we might make. Maren, this is no longer about legacy. It is no longer bigger than the two of us. It is us. Us and our children. And if I deny us, it is because I'm carrying on the legacy of pain. I do not wish to do that. Not to you, not to the children. Not to myself. It is simply not worth it. Nothing is worth the cost of losing you. Nothing. I want… I want your love. And you did not ever have to worry about whether or not I love you enough. I am miserable without you. You should've seen me while I was away."

"Why did you stay away for so long?"

"I was trying to prove to myself that this was still about legacy. That it was about the way I could control the world around me. That it wasn't about feelings for me. Because how could it be? I had thought always that I was fated to marry into the Argos family. I had never thought that I could have love. Because nothing in my life was about it. I realize that now. I thought that it was. I thought I was motivated by my love for my mother, and that she survived because of my love for her. But it is not that. I simply gave her what she wanted. I thought that love was the cage. But it's greed. Greed is an endless well of dissatisfaction. And that is my mother's real problem. You were right. All along. And you are right about this too. I don't need to live in this palace. I want to give our children a good life. A life with friends. A life surrounded by love. Because that is truly what matters. I want them to understand that our love for them is based on nothing like giving to us."

"Acastus," she whispered, putting her hand on his

face. "Thank you for showing me this place. Now let's leave. Because this is not us. And you're free."

"Yes," he said, his voice hard. "We are."

"My love is free," she said. "I don't need a palace. I don't need glorious stained glass windows, or marble halls. I don't need pristine seas and an endless closet and being a princess. I need you. Your love. You are my joy. Just as you are."

He held her tightly, afraid his heart might burst. Afraid he might unravel.

Finally, he spoke, around a tightness in his throat that was nearly unbearable. "You are my heart. And I… It is the strangest thing. I feel like I am no longer carrying the burden I once did. I feel like…"

"I want to be with you. Carrying all the emotions you have. Whether they're sweet or sour, or sharp or soft. I'm yours. You're mine. And this is love."

"Yes, love," he said, because all other words were beyond him.

They walked out, and went to the room, where they dressed.

And then they went into the study for their Christmas morning. And there were presents, piled high, but as lovely as they were, they weren't what really mattered.

What mattered was her. What mattered was love.

And he would never have to question if what they had was enough. Because it was everything.

He sat there with her, his hand on her stomach,

their future before them. More interesting than anything left in her past.

And she kissed him on the mouth. "And they lived happily ever after."

# EPILOGUE

THE NEXT CHRISTMAS was bright and glorious.

He and Maren had bought a house near Jessie and Ewan in Scotland, and they also had one in Greece for when they wished to go to sunny weather. But at Christmastime, they had all decided that the castle was the place to go.

The twins—Athena and Diophantus—were sitting crabbily beneath the Christmas tree, overwhelmed by the festivities, while their cousin toddled around them.

It was a warmth and happiness like Acastus had never known. Ewan had truly become like a brother to him, Jessie a very real sister.

Family was something he was beginning to understand in a way he never had. And love could never be a cage. Love, and his new experience, was an ever-expanding resource. One that grew exponentially with each passing year. Every time one of his children did something new. Every time they looked at him. Every time Maren kissed him, or smiled.

He had told her once that he sometimes felt like he had a grave responsibility to her because she remembered everything.

"It's funny," she responded. "Because it matters less and less. My memory. What matters most of all is what I feel. And every day with you I simply feel loved."

Love, he was discovering, was enough in all cases.

"A real Christmas present to you," Jessie said, grinning, "is the news that we are having another baby."

"Oh, good," said Acastus. "Then you'll finally understand the trials and tribulations of having two."

They laughed.

And when he took Maren to bed that night she looked at him sheepishly. "It is entirely possible that nine months from now, you and I will understand the trials and tribulations of three."

He stared at his wife. "You're joking. The twins aren't even six months old."

"I know. Someone needs to talk to my husband about it."

He smiled, and he felt the love inside of him grow yet again.

"The problem," he said. "Is that your husband is desperately in love with you."

"I don't consider it a problem," she whispered. "In fact, it's the greatest joy of my life."

\* \* \* \* \*

*If you fell in love with*
The Christmas the Greek Claimed Her
*don't forget to check out the first installment in the*
*From Destitute to Diamonds duet*
The Billionaire's Accidental Legacy

*And why not also explore these*
*other Millie Adams stories?*

Crowning His Innocent Assistant
The Only King to Claim Her
His Secretly Pregnant Cinderella
The Billionaire's Baby Negotiation
A Vow to Set the Virgin Free

*Available now!*

## #4153 THE MAID'S PREGNANCY BOMBSHELL
*Cinderella Sisters for Billionaires*
by Lynne Graham

Shy hotel maid Alana is so desperate to clear a family debt that when she discovers Greek tycoon Ares urgently needs a wife, she blurts out a scandalous suggestion: *she'll* become his convenient bride. But as chemistry blazes between them, she has an announcement that will inconveniently disrupt his well-ordered world... She's having his baby!

## #4154 A BILLION-DOLLAR HEIR FOR CHRISTMAS
by Caitlin Crews

When Tiago Villela discovers Lillie Merton is expecting, a wedding is nonnegotiable. To protect the Villela billions, his child must be legitimate. But his plan for a purely pragmatic arrangement is soon threatened by a dangerously insatiable desire...

## #4155 A CHRISTMAS CONSEQUENCE FOR THE GREEK
*Heirs to a Greek Empire*
by Lucy King

Booking billionaire Zander's birthday is a triumph for caterer Mia. And the hottest thing on the menu? A scorching one-night stand! But a month later, he can't be reached. Mia finally ambushes him at work to reveal she's pregnant! He insists she move in with him, but this Christmas she wants all or nothing!

## #4156 MISTAKEN AS HIS ROYAL BRIDE
*Princess Brides for Royal Brothers*
by Abby Green

Maddi hadn't fully considered the implications of posing as her secret half sister. *Or* that King Aristedes would demand she continue the pretense as his intended bride. Immersing herself in the royal life she was denied growing up is as compelling as it is daunting. But so is the thrill of Aristedes's smoldering gaze...

### #4157 VIRGIN'S STOLEN NIGHTS WITH THE BOSS
*Heirs to the Romero Empire*
by Carol Marinelli

Polo player Elias rarely spares a glance for his staff, until he meets stable hand and former heiress Carmen. And their attraction is irresistible! Elias knows he'll give the innocent all the pleasure she could want, but that's it. Unless their passion can unlock a connection much harder to walk away from...

### #4158 CROWNED FOR THE KING'S SECRET
*Behind the Palace Doors...*
by Kali Anthony

One year ago, her spine-tingling night with exiled king Sandro left Victoria pregnant and alone. Lied to by the palace, she believed he wanted nothing to do with them. So Sandro turning up on her doorstep—ready to claim her, his heir and his kingdom—is astounding!

### #4159 HIS INNOCENT UNWRAPPED IN ICELAND
by Jackie Ashenden

Orion North wants Isla's company...and her! So when the opportunity to claim both at the convenient altar arises, he takes it. But with tragedy in his past, even their passion may not be enough to melt the ice encasing his heart...

### #4160 THE CONVENIENT COSENTINO WIFE
by Jane Porter

Clare Redmond retreated from the world, pregnant and grieving her fiancé's death, never expecting to see his ice-cold brother, Rocco, again. She's stunned when the man who always avoided her storms back into her life, demanding they wed to give her son the life a Cosentino deserves!

---

**YOU CAN FIND MORE INFORMATION ON UPCOMING HARLEQUIN TITLES, FREE EXCERPTS AND MORE AT HARLEQUIN.COM.**

HPCNMRB1023

# Get 3 FREE REWARDS!

**We'll send you 2 FREE Books plus a FREE Mystery Gift.**

**FREE** Value Over **$20**

Both the **Harlequin®** Desire and **Harlequin Presents®** series feature compelling novels filled with passion, sensuality and intriguing scandals.